Young God

Amelia Douglas

Contents

Prologue

"How can you be so sure you'll be in love with me for the rest of your life?"

"Because I just know."

Chapter 1

I walked through the doors of my school with my uniform skirt brushing against my pale legs. Our school uniform consisted of a tacky white button up, blazer with our school's logo, and a mid-thigh, navy school skirt or the ugliest pair of bootcut navy slacks. I paired it with my ruffled white ankle socks and a pair of white Gucci sneakers. My mid back, dark brown hair was pulled into a half-up, half-down style with hairs pulled out to frame my face. My dark lashes coated in black mascara brought out my green eyes and the contour I applied this morning helped accentuate my cheekbones.

It was the first day back from winter break and here I was, the second semester of my junior year. Of course, I was freezing, but being cold in my skirt beats having to wear the hideous pants that are allowed in our school uniforms.

My back was already killing me from all the textbooks that I was required to carry at Prestige High School. The high school was filled with elites from all over the world, but the main campus was located here, in New York. These elites included kids of movie actors and actresses, senators, millionaires, basically the best of the best. My father owned a law firm while my mother owned her own luxury clothing line, and so this school was the one they decided to enroll me in.

Walking through the halls made me sick thinking of the schoolwork and homework that I would be stuck with until summer finally came. However, on the bright side, I did see my best friends already standing by my locker gossiping away.

"My mom ended up inviting Brandon's girlfriend with us to the French Alps and it sucked because she's a total snob," said Claire while flipping her blonde hair over her shoulder and rolling her dark green eyes. Claire was taller than the rest of us and had beautiful tanned skin. Her mom used to be a popular model, so Claire was following in her mother's footsteps.

"Since when does Brandon have a girlfriend?" I asked walking up to my friends with a smile on my face.

"Well, well, well. Welcome back Aria, did you have a pleasant time in Bora Bora over break?" smirked my other best friend Elena, who had black hair that flowed down her waist and dark brown eyes that followed her tan complexion. Elena was the same height as me, reaching about 5'7, and her father owned his own tech company, but she hated anything to do with math and computers.

"Well they're not together anymore, and what the hell Aria. How do you spend a whole week on the beach and not get any darker?" Claire asked me sarcastically.

I rolled my eyes, "I've told you ladies a million times that I can't tan to save my life."

"Anyways, can we talk about the fact that this break passed by way too quickly," said my third and final best friend Victoria, who had short blonde hair that stopped at her shoulders and bright blue eyes. She was the shortest out of all four of us, and she was just as pale as I was. Her dad was a heart surgeon and her mother was a plastic surgeon, which allowed her access to any plastic surgery she could ever want, though she hadn't gotten any yet.

"Dude I feel that I can't wait for another semester full of no boys wanting to get within a 5-foot radius of me," I said rolling my eyes. I never thought that I was ugly, but maybe it was time to start considering that possibility.

"Maybe it's for the best that you don't have one. Don't feel bad about it, at least you're not ugly," Claire said patting me on the shoulder. Well, at least I didn't have to worry about being ugly anymore.

We went on chatting about all the things we did over break and how unhappy we were to be back at school.

My friends and I were apart of the top level of kids at our school, so we were some of the more popular girls here. I honestly could care less about this "title" we've obtained, but my friends loved it and I loved them so I dealt with it. At my high school, there's a social hierarchy, and although the kids here were elites, some were just richer and more prestige than others and considering that my parents were well known, I just happened to be in the top tier.

We had some time to kill before class started so in between catching up and going through social media, we were learning some of the juiciest gossip.

"Oh my God," Elena said looking up from her phone. "Leonardo Moretti is coming back this semester."

This gossip, in particular, happened to be extra juicy so we were in for a treat.

Leonardo Moretti was the son of billionaire Steven Moretti who just so happened to also be the leader of the Italian Mafia. Rumors had it that his son Leonardo was following in his footsteps and was quite possibly more feared than his own father. He was ruthless and I intended to stay as far away from him as I possibly could.

"No way, I thought his dad sent him to Italy to go to a boarding school?" I asked Elena confused.

"He did, but I guess he's back. I'll find out whatever I can and I'll get back to you guys with the deets." Leave it to Elena to find out the latest information.

The bell rang signaling that it was time for class, so we began walking. Victoria and I had english right in the morning together so we typically walked to class together. We sat down at our table and waited for the teacher to begin teaching.

Majority of the conversations going on in class were surrounding the whole situation with Leonardo's return. I overheard a conversation behind me from Rachel and another girl who I've never really talked to.

"I heard that he's coming back because he got in trouble in Italy, so the school kicked him out. Makes sense considering that he never really wanted to leave in the first place," I heard Rachel say.

The other girl scoffed, "Please, are you kidding me? They would never kick Steven Moretti's son out of anywhere," she had a good point there. "I heard that he came back for something but no one really knows what."

"Oh my god, what if it's a person? I hope that it's me!" Rachel excitedly said. I rolled my eyes, this was the point when I stopped listening.

"Dude everyone's going crazy over this whole Leonardo situation," I told Victoria.

"I know, but I guess when you're that feared and rich, people are bound to care about what happens in your life," Victoria shrugged, opening her book up to the pages written on the board.

I opened my book up as well but I couldn't stop thinking about Leonardo.

Why did he come back?

Chapter 2

The next couple of classes passed by and before I knew it, it was lunch time. Also considered as my favorite time because there are no teachers lecturing and I get to eat. What more can a person want in life?

Victoria, Elena, Claire, and I all sat down at our usual table after grabbing food. One of the many perks of our school was that they had amazing food, but considering how much we had to pay to be here I wouldn't accept anything less.

We were chatting about any weekend plans we had while eating our lunches when the doors opened up and the whole cafeteria turned dead silent. I turned my head to see what the commotion was all about. It was Leonardo Moretti and his posse.

His inner circle friend group consisted of Damon Rossi who was the closest to Leonardo, and whose father happened to be Steven Moretti's (Leonardo's father's) second in command. He had light brown hair that was slightly curly and dark green eyes. Damon was certainly in very good shape and easy on the eyes.

Next was Justin Smalls whose father owned an oil company, he was more on the lanky side but was really smart. He had blonde hair and dark blue eyes, with freckles that covered his cheeks. I used to have a couple of classes with him last year and he was always really nice.

Then there was Vince Marino whose father was an extremely popular surgeon around the country. He was following in his father's footsteps and had an eye for anything medical related. He had short black hair and hazel eyes that complimented his dark skin very well. Vince was also very fit and had been nice to me ever since freshman year.

Lastly, there was Leonardo Moretti. He was the tallest out of the four and looked like he was around 6'2. He had dark, jet black hair and the iciest blue eyes I had ever seen. He walked with confidence and his built arms had become littered with tattoos. There was no doubt that he was attractive, but the feared attitude he gave off stopped all girls from coming after him. At only 17 years old, he was feared by both older and younger men and women, but my God was he hot.

"Holy crap, I was not expecting to see him today," said Elena with her mouth open in shock replicating everyone else's faces in the cafeteria. I nodded my head in agreement.

"Oh my god Justin is so hot," Claire said while sighing.

"Claire now is not the time," Victoria rolled her eyes.

It looked like Leonardo was looking around and his eyes squinted ever so slightly as if he was looking for something in specific before they finally landed on something. Me. We made eye contact and I saw him faintly smirk before him and his friends started walking over to our table.

"Oh my god are they walking over here? Aria why did you look him in the eye!" Elena whisper shouted.

"I have no idea, what do we do?" My eyes wide, I started panicking.

Claire looked like she was going to pass out, before Victoria cut in, "Maybe they're not even coming to our table? Maybe they just have to walk this way to pass by. Everyone act calm."

Next thing I knew, the four of them stood in front of our table with Leonardo in the front leading them. My heart literally stopped.

"Hello Aria," Leonardo said looking at me directly in the eye. His voice was rough and deep, and he made my name sound amazing rolling off of his tongue.

I forgot how to breathe, I could feel the whole school looking at me.

"H-Hi," I cursed myself for stuttering but I had literally never felt more awkward in my entire life.

A faint smile appeared on his lips upon hearing my voice, "How have you been?"

"Um good- great, yeah. Welcome back," I said offering him a small smile. Why did I say that? Maybe it was a sensitive topic? I mean sure our parents know each other considering that my father handled some of his father's cases, but we're not at that level of closeness that I could bring up stuff like that.

"I certainly am happier now," he said while still holding eye contact. I could see my friends refusing to look at Leonardo. He didn't allow anyone to look him in the eye and yet here I was, literally holding eye contact, practically asking for a death wish.

I cleared my voice, "I'm glad to hear that." I began to look down at the table hoping he would leave.

"I was actually going to ask if I could walk you to your next class."

I looked up quickly, my eyes wide. Did he really just ask to walk me to class? Why? We hardly talked before he went to Italy and we didn't talk while he was in Italy, so why the hell was he asking to walk me to class?

"Oh um ha, sure," I said trying to act cool. In reality, my heart was beating so quick and my palms were becoming more and more sweaty. I was having a mini panic attack but it's fine, just someone really attractive and really freaking scary wanting to walk me to class. No biggie.

"Great," he said smirking at me. I began to get up, grabbing my bag as I got up. I looked at my friends who all had shocked faces and their mouth's dropped.

I walked around the table to meet up with him, with my backpack hanging off of one of my shoulders. Before I could put the other strap on, I felt his hand grab the backpack off of my shoulder and he held it in his hands. I was even more shocked than before and I think everyone else was too. Leonardo literally did not talk to any girl ever, hell I don't think he's ever dated a girl before, and here he was doing something as simple as carrying the backpack of a girl he never talks to.

"Alright let's go," he said placing the backpack over his shoulder. I felt the warmth of his hand on my lower back as he began leading me out the cafeteria doors.

What the hell did I get myself into?

Chapter 3

The beginning of the walk was incredibly awkward. I think this had to do with the fact that I was keeping my distance from Leonardo, but in my defense, this man was pretty terrifying. I could feel him trying to get closer and closer to me, but I just kept moving more and more away from him.

"So what class do you have coming up?" he asked breaking the silence between us. Considering the fact that lunch didn't end for another five minutes, we had some time to spare so I wasn't all that much in a rush to get to class.

"Oh I have chemistry," I said while reciting my schedule in my head. He nodded his head and we kept walking.

"It's been a while since I've last seen you," he told me while turning his head to look at me. I could feel his eyes staring into the side of my head, but I kept my eyes glued to the floor keeping my focus on my shoes.

"You left for a little while there." I really don't think my head processes the majority of the things that come out of my mouth.

I finally mustered up the courage to look at him, just to have him looking back at me. Our eyes locked and immediately I could feel my heart rate picking up.

He smirked me, "It was the longest two years of my life being away from you."

My eyes widened and I felt my cheeks getting hot, I immediately looked back at the ground. How the hell do I respond to that? Did Leonardo have feelings for me? A million thoughts were running through my head and yet I still couldn't think of an appropriate response to his question.

The only thing that came out of my mouth was a squeaked, "What?"

"Aria, there's a lot of things you have yet to know, but in due time everything will be revealed. Patience is key little one," he told me grabbing my hand to make us stop walking. I hadn't noticed that we had already gotten to the class, those three minutes felt like a lifetime with him.

His rough hand reached under my chin and lifted my head up so that we were face to face. I hadn't noticed how close he had gotten to me, and now his body was a mere couple inches away from mine.

"I-wha-I don-," I began before he shushed me.

"I have some things I need to take care of, however, after your class, I will pick you up and we will drive home together. I do believe that our parents are having dinner later tonight, so makes more sense to go together," he smiled at me before letting go of my hand and walking away from me, leaving my flabbergasted self, standing in front of the class. At this point, lunch had already ended and kids were beginning to make their way to class, most of them looking at me with either curiosity or a look of shock. It might've been both but I'm sure that my face resembled the same look.

I still had no idea what was going on but when I walked into class, all I could think about was being in a car alone with Leonardo and how did he know what my last class of the day was?

Plus the fact that his family and my family were having dinner together tonight, it all just seemed like everything was moving a little bit too quickly for me to wrap my head around. I mean all in one day I heard he was back, and then suddenly he's walking me to class and then we're driving home together. What the hell was going on?

I went to my seat and waited for the rest of the class to fill up. I had to tell the girls about everything that happened because I honestly did not know what to think of it all.

As the teacher began her lecture, I still was not able to focus on any of the information she was talking about as my mind was filled with thoughts of the blue eyes I had come into contact with today. I really needed to chill out.

All I could think about was one thing.

What did Leonardo want with me?

----

sorry for the short chapter, the next one is a long one!

Chapter 4

I was keeping track of the minutes until my chemistry class ended and my anxiety was peeking at every minute that passed by. I had texted the girls telling them everything that happened while Leonardo walked me to class, and they were all pretty shocked and just as confused as I was.

I had given myself a pep talk in order to establish some sort of confidence, while in the presence of Leonardo later. I had to stop being a nervous wreck and stand tall and proud. Given the fact that I was quite awkward around people naturally, especially around a person of the opposite sex who was both incredibly attractive and intimidating as Leonardo, this was a huge step up.

Typically during class, I would find myself dozing off considering that history, to me, was extremely boring. However, the nervous feeling I had in the pit of my stomach stopped me from being able to do that. I wasn't ready for whatever was going to happen after this class ended.

My teacher gave us a worksheet to complete during the last ten minutes of the class, but at this rate, I was probably going to have to finish it for homework.

Soon enough, the bell rang and my heart literally dropped. I took my time packing up my things in hopes that I could postpone the interaction between Leonardo and I for as long as possible. Eventually, I had to leave the class and be a big girl.

I walked out and noticed Leonardo waiting outside, leaning against the lockers. He smirked as soon as he saw me, and this time I held eye contact with him instead of shying away.

"Are you ready to go?" I asked him.

He seemed a little bit shocked, probably because I was initiating the conversation first, but nonetheless, he nodded his head and said, "Let's go, my driver is out front waiting."

He gestured for me to walk first and so I did, but he soon was walking right beside me. The hallway cleared as soon as everyone saw us walking together, all shocked seeing that it was clearly not a one-time occurrence of Leonardo walking with me.

I was embarrassed to be the center of attention like this, and I wanted to hide from all of the prying eyes. I felt Leo walk closer next to me and when I looked up at him, he had yet again another smirk on his face. Feeling my eyes on the side of his face, he turned his head to look at me, but I quickly looked away from him feeling my cheeks get hotter.

Thankfully the walk from my class to the front doors wasn't that long, and in no time we were already outside where his driver was waiting with the car.

"Good afternoon Mr. Moretti and Miss. Moon," his driver said while opening the doors for us. I thanked him before getting into the car first, Leo soon following in after me. I let out a sigh as soon as I was engulfed by the heat of the car.

The back seat of the car was huge and yet it felt so small with Leonardo's big frame covering the majority of it.

It seemed that the more I scooched away from him, the closer he would come to me. However, him being this close to me, I was able to smell his cologne and it had to be the best scent I had ever smelt in my life. Something about boys cologne was amazing, but his, in particular, was heaven.

However, I was not going to let this delicious smelling man beside me distract me from getting the answers to all the questions I had for him. The only problem was that I had no idea how to bring the topic up in this silent car.

That was until I felt his body turn towards me and he cleared his throat, "So how was school today?"

I shifted my body slightly so that I was faced towards him a little better, "It was alright, it's school, it can't be all that good, right?" I tried to crack a joke, in order to help ease the slight awkwardness in the car.

It seemed to work, especially when I heard him let out a small chuckle. "That it certainly is."

This was my chance to begin asking some questions. "So you mentioned that our families were having dinner together tonight?"

"Ah yes, my father arranged it last minute, like he does most things," he whispered the last part more to himself, but I still managed to hear it.

"Oh, nice." Time to ask my next question. "How did you enjoy Italy, I bet it was beautiful out there." That's it Aria, little questions and hopefully, we can find out some more information.

"It certainly was, unfortunately, I had to leave something else here that was far more beautiful," he had his little smirk on his face again when he said that.

"Oh okay," I told him with a confused look on my face. I wonder what was more beautiful here than in Italy, so I asked him, "like what?

His smirk got bigger, "Now that is a secret."

Hmm, this was going to be slightly more difficult than I entailed, especially if he doesn't tell me anything. "Okay then, what made you decide to come back?"

"Well, in a couple of years I will be taking over my father's position so he wants me to work with him a lot more now, and of course that thing I mentioned earlier."

My eyes widened at his statement, "A couple of years? That's really young."

His face turned more serious at my comment, maybe my question overstepped the boundaries? "I'm sorry you don't have to talk about it, just forget I said anything," I said quickly jerking my body away from him, trying to bury myself into the seat of the car. I was embarrassed and now I was going to pay for making such an inappropriate comment.

"Aria," I felt his hand grab my shoulder, "I'm not angry at you, I don't even think I could ever be mad at you. Come on, turn back around."

I slowly started turning my body back towards him, but I was still cautious of him. I looked into his eyes and saw what seemed like worry in them. Why was Leonardo being so nice to me and what did he mean by his last comment?

Before I could ask him about it, he beat me to it. "My father believes that I have what it takes to run our business. I'm both respected and feared by many, in the mafia business that's a key skill to have and yet many still are not able to get it. I, at 17 years old, have both." He looked proud of himself, but I guess that's a good thing especially considering what he's going to be doing for the rest of his life. "And please Aria, don't ever hide from me like that, you are the only person in the world that should never fear me."

He spoke in a tone that was so serious and absolute. Yet I still had to ask the question, "Why are you so nice to me?"

"I will have to answer that question later on little one because looks like we have arrived at your house," he told me.

I looked out the window and sure enough, we had arrived. For some reason, I was kind of sad that our time was up.

But I needed to know, why was Leonardo the exact opposite of what everyone said about him?

Chapter 5

The driver opened the door for us and Leonardo got out first. He offered a hand out for me as I was getting out of the car, so I grabbed it but quickly let go of it as soon as my feet were on the ground again. His expression changed to something I couldn't pinpoint, but it quickly went back to be emotionless soon after. However, I didn't dwell on it for too long, there were much more pressing matters that I had to attend to at the moment.

We walked up to the door with Leonardo carrying my backpack yet again. I just walked in considering that I lived there, with Leo trailing behind me.

"Mom, dad?" I called out assuming that they were home considering they were preparing for the dinner.

"In the kitchen sweetheart," I heard my mom's voice and I nudged my head for Leonardo to follow me.

We walked to the kitchen and it seemed like a mess. There were cooks everywhere preparing food, people were setting up the table with the nicest china, it was all a bit much considering that this was a dinner between six people.

"Hi mom, this is a bit much don't you think?" I asked her referring to the chaos of the kitchen.

"Nonsense honey, I just want everything to be perfect for later," she told me before her eyes locked on the incredibly large boy standing behind me. "Oh my God, Leonardo is that you? I haven't seen you in forever, my God you have grown so much. Oh and so handsome too," she gushed while pulling him into a hug.

He looked stunned at first before accepting her hug, "It's good to see you again Mrs. Moon," he told her while pulling away from the hug.

"Oh please call me Lauren," she looked down to the watch on her hand, "Gosh you guys are early, dinner won't be starting for another hour, Aria why don't you go show Leonardo around the house, you guys could go to the theater room!" She smiled at me, but I knew this wasn't up for debate.

I squinted my eyes at her, "Sure mom, cmon Leonardo, we'll stop at my room first."

I led him through the living room and up the stairs before going down the hall to the last door on the left. We walked in and immediately was welcomed by my happy place. My room was decorated around the color yellow, and honestly, it was very aesthetically pleasing. My mom hired a well known interior designer who put together the room of my dreams. The bed was huge and had white comforters and lots of pillows that were decorated with whites and yellow. My closet was huge, but because my mother was a fashion designer, I had no choice but to love fashion as well and I needed enough storage to fit it all. Lastly was my ensuite bathroom that had white marble flooring, gold accents, and a huge shower.

"Cute room," he said while putting my backpack on the table next to the door, before walking over to my bed and sitting down.

I took off my blazer, placing it on my desk chair. "Thank you."

"Come sit next to me," he said patting the spot next to him.

I walked over and sat down on the far end of the bed keeping some space between the two of us.

He smirked, "You can come closer, I won't bite."

I hesitantly moved closer next to him, content with the space between us. That was until I felt his hands grab my waist and pull me closer to him until our legs and shoulders were touching. A squeak left my mouth at the sudden movement and I felt my face get red for what seemed like the thousandth time today.

His smirk seemed like it got even bigger, "There, now we're good."

Now that we were alone, this was my chance to get some answers from him. The house tour would have to wait until later.

"Leo can I ask-" I began but was quickly cut off.

"What did you call me?" he asked me with an amused look in his eyes.

My face was flushed and I couldn't understand what the big deal was, "Leonard-"

"No, what did you call me before?"

"Leo-"

"I've never had anyone that wasn't my parents call me anything other than Leonardo, but I do like that nickname coming from your mouth." He told me and although the joking tone was there, I knew that he was being serious.

"Okay," I said trying to get us back onto the topic we were on before, which was me getting some answers. "Now that we're alone, you can answer my question from before."

However, Leo seemed to want to continue joking around because he wasn't taking me seriously. "Could you please refresh my memory from before? I don't seem to recall any question being asked." His eyes were full of amusement and he seemed to love making me all squirmy and uncomfortable.

I stood my ground and wasn't going to let him distract me from my answers and I raised my eyebrows, "I asked you earlier why you were so nice to me."

He thought about it for a second, "Why do you think I'm so nice to you?"

Are you kidding me? Why was he so frustrating?

I rolled my eyes, "Don't try to flip this around like that. If it's not a big deal why don't you just answer my question then?" I got up to stand in front of him and I crossed my arms over my chest.

He got up as well and began taking slow steps towards me, all amusement that was there once before was gone and replaced with a look of challenge. "Who said it wasn't a big deal?" he asked me while walking closer to me. The more steps he took towards me, the more steps I took backwards trying to put some distance between us.

I don't think that Leo was trying to keep any distance between us, because soon enough my back hit the edge of the desk. He placed his arms on both sides of me, trapping me in. He leaned down so that his face was directly in front of mine and I stopped breathing. His lips were inches away from mine and for some reason, I couldn't stop looking at them. Even weirder was that I wanted to see what they felt like on mine. I don't know why I was having these thoughts, especially about Leo.

"And maybe I quite enjoy seeing you become all hot and flustered trying to get answers from me, but I think you and I both know that you know why I'm so nice to you," his face leaned in and I felt his lips so close to my ear. He whispered, "It's because you're m-"

Before he could finish, he was interrupted by a knock at the door. I quickly pushed him away from me, my body feeling much cooler without his practically on top of me.

I cleared my throat before answering, "Come in!" I smoothed out my skirt quickly and tried to make the red on my cheeks disappear.

The door opened and I recognized it as one of the women that work around the house for my parents, "Miss. Moon, you both have been summoned into the dining room."

"Thank you, Mrs. Smith, we are on the way down," I told her with a smile. She closed the door shortly after and I was again left with Leo.

He walked towards the door and opened it, "After you sweetheart," he held it open for me. I walked through but not before his hand grabbed mine stopping me. His face leaned in again and I felt his lips right next to my ear before whispering, "Maybe we can finish our conversation later."

My face turned even redder and instead of answering, I just walked away hurrying to get away from him. My body was hot and I needed to cool down before facing his family and mine. I felt him walking behind me, and all I could think about was how much I enjoyed him being so close to me for some weird reason.

Why did I enjoy Leo being so close to me?

I never mentioned this before but if you are enjoying the story leave a vote or a comment! I would love to see what you guys think about it!

Chapter 6

Once we got downstairs I saw the four adults standing by the table with cocktails in their hands. The moment we entered the dining room, the conversation stopped and they all turned to look at Leo and I.

One woman, who I was assuming was Leo's mother walked towards us first. "Hello Aria, it's so good to see you. Look at you, such a beautiful woman now," she told me pulling me into a hug.

I hugged her back, "You look amazing as well Mrs. Moretti." It was true. She looked very young for her age and she had hair to her shoulders that was dark like Leo's. Her eyes were a dark, chocolate brown and she was quite short compared to Leo, but a little bit taller than me. She was wearing a red, professional dress and heels along with pearls all along her neck.

"Now now sweetheart, we're practically family, please call me Sofia," she told me with a warm smile on her face. A look of confusion crossed my face at the mention of being family but went away quickly. She probably meant that since our families were so close, we were like family.

My eyes then moved to the person behind her. Leo's father. He was a big man like Leo and was still in incredible shape despite his age. Leo got a majority of his looks from Steven, and probably got the imitation gene from him as well. Steven had icy blue eyes much like his son, and he was sporting a very nice suit. The Mafia Don himself was standing in front of me.

I reached out my hand for him to shake, "Don Moretti, it's nice to see you again."

He let out a little laugh, "Cmon hon, you can call me Steven. Like my wife said we're practically family, come give me a hug," he said to me with his arms open.

I hesitantly walked towards him and hugged him back. His hold was strong and he probably didn't mean it, but damn I was delicate.

I was still so confused at their mention of being family but that quickly left my mind as soon as I saw Leo talking to my father. My dad seemed to have a stern look on his face but I could see in his eyes there was admiration. I had no idea what they were talking about, but I don't think I wanted to know either.

"Alright everyone, why don't we go ahead and sit down at the table to eat?" my mom asked and everyone began sitting down.

As I was going to pull out my own chair to sit, someone else grabbed it from me and pulled it out. I looked behind me and saw that it was Leo. I instantly felt my face become redder by the second and I could feel the eyes of all of the adults on us. I sat on the chair and murmured a quiet 'thank you' while he pushed my chair in. I kept my eyes drawn to the table instead of everyone that was there.

Leonardo took the seat next to me, and when I gained the courage to look up again I saw that everyone was still looking at us. My mom and Sofia had huge smiles on their faces, while Steven sported a look of pride. My dad had his eyes squinted and pointed towards Leo but I don't think he realized because his eyes were still trained on me.

The table was a large rectangle and my parents sat on either end of the table with Leo and I on one side, and his parents on the other. Sofia and I were on the sides closest to my mom while the boys were on the side closest to my dad.

I grabbed the napkin from the plate and placed it on my lap like I was taught to do from all those etiquette lessons I was forced to take in order to learn proper tableside manners. I felt Leo's eyes drilling into the side of my head as I did this.

"Why do you keep staring at me?" I murmured to him.

"Because I want to," he said with a smirk on his face.

I rolled my eyes and tried to ignore the boy next to me and instead focus on the conversations going on around me. Soon enough, the food was brought out and my mouth watered at the sight of it. So much had occupied my mind today that I completely forgot to have a snack like I usually would after school. However, now was the time for me to feast.

There was chicken, mashed potatoes, veggies, steak, and the best bread I had ever tasted in my life. The dinner wouldn't have been complete without other things that were too fancy for my liking and as a picky person, I decided not to try them. I piled a little bit of everything onto my plate and began eating, but I again felt eyes drilling into my soul.

I turned my head with my eyes squinted at Leo, "What?"

He looked at me and let out a light chuckle, "I like a woman that can eat."

"I like a woman that can eat," I mocked him rolling my eyes and went back to my food.

Quickly, however, I was pulled out of my peaceful eating and into what seemed like the game 21 questions by Leo's parents.

"So Aria," Sofia began, "what are your plans after you finish high school."

I took a sip of my lemonade, "I'm going to go to college while interning for my mom to one day join her in the fashion industry." I smiled at my mom and I saw the look of pride in her eyes staring back at me. My mom had been happy when I told her that I wanted to follow her route of becoming a fashion designer instead of becoming a lawyer like my dad.

"Oh that's wonderful sweetheart, you'd make an amazing designer. So any guys at the moment?" she asked me innocently, but there seemed to be more to her question. I saw Leo stiffen up at her question through my peripheral vision.

I nearly choked on my food, but quickly regained my composure, "Um no, not at the moment."

At my response, I saw Leo's tense figure become more relaxed, and his mom began to giggle, "Oh I'm sure that'll change soon." She winked at me.

Before I could ask her what she meant by that, my mom jumped into the conversation, "So Leonardo, how was the school in Italy. It must've been very beautiful out there."

Leo cleared his throat, "It was a very gorgeous setting indeed, I just really missed being home."

"We thought that it was best for Leonardo to get a better feel in Italy of the things he'll be doing once he takes over the business," Steven cut in.

I could see Leonardo become upset at his dad, but I couldn't understand why. I mean it seems like it was a good opportunity for him to gain some experience.

"Of course dad, you seem to know everything that's best for me," Leo sneered at his dad, "I begged you to let me stay, but next thing I know I'm on a jet." He stood up abruptly, his chair flying from behind him. He stormed out of the room slamming the door behind him.

I had never seen Leo this upset and it made me kind of fear him. There was an awkward silence that followed afterward and I could tell that both Sofia and Steven were embarrassed by his actions.

I should've just stayed in my seat and not intervened, but something in me told me to get up and follow Leo to see if he was alright.

"I'm gonna go check on him," I told all of the adults before placing the napkin that was in my lap on the table and leaving the dining room.

I looked all over the first floor before I noticed the back door slightly opened to the back yard. I opened it slightly and saw Leo sitting on the patio couch with his head in his hands.

"Hey Leo," I said softly not wanting to alarm his already upset state. It was freezing outside and I had no idea how he was sitting outside in it for so long.

He looked up from his hands and again patted the spot next to him. I slowly walked over and took the seat, turning my body slightly towards him.

"Do you wanna talk about it?" I asked him.

For a few moments, it was silent before I heard his raspy voice begin to talk, "I didn't want to go to Italy."

Before I could ask questions he continued talking, "My dad forced me to go, one day he told me and the next I was gone. I had to leave everything behind here. Everything. He won't tell anyone this but he kept me in charge of the business in Italy. The things I saw, it destroys a person. The things I had to do, they were all awful. You would think that it would break me down but it didn't. The power I had through the fear I emitted, it made me thirsty, thirsty for more. I was hungry for the power, for the complete and total control I had over everyone. I had completely changed and I loved it. People fear me now, and they'll fear me even more once I'm actually the Don. I was just a kid when I left, but I grew up real quick. I was a new person, and yet there was one part of me that remained the same. It was the part of my heart that you had control over and you didn't even know it. I could forgive him for making me into a monster, for making me the power-hungry man I am. However, I could never forgive him for taking me away from the only person that matters to me. You."

He looked me straight in the eyes and I held my breath. I didn't know how to react or what to say, but this confirmed everything I had assumed thus far. Leo had feelings for me.

"Why me?" I asked him.

"It was when I saw you for the first time at your father's law firm when you were around eight years old. I was also eight at the time, but my father wanted me to begin getting a grasp at everything that involved the business and that included meeting the man who handled all of my father's legal trouble. That moment I saw you, I knew there was something special about you. You were beautiful then and you're even more beautiful now. But I had to be patient and wait until you were ready to understand. Once I was forced to leave for Italy, I made sure to have guards posted around to keep you safe and especially keep all unwanted males away from you. This is all I can tell you for now. Things tend to work differently in my family and one day when you're ready I'll tell you, but for now you'll just have to wait." he said.

"Whoa, whoa, whoa, wait! What the hell? You have barely talked to me and yet you have this crush on me? Then, out of nowhere, you begin to show this interest in me? It doesn't make sense." Leo had to be the most confusing person in the world.

Before he could respond however I remembered something else he said, "And your guards did what! You hired people to keep boys away from me? For what reason? Oh my God, is this what your parents meant earlier? Did they know about this crush you had on me?" I asked him almost yelling at this point. I was confused.

He sighed, "Well first off, I couldn't handle myself. I hadn't seen you in two years, that is two too many, so my instincts seemed to kick in and I had to find you. I had waited too long, and after all, I am an impatient man Aria. And of course my parents knew, you are the reason for my return after all.

And for that other part, you're mine and I didn't want any little boys around you. Period." He said venomously with jealousy laced in his voice. From seeing the many sides of Leo today, this one had to be the one that was the worst.

"I'm what? No, I'm not yours, you can't just put some kind of claim on me like that. Who do you think you are? You can't tell me who I can and can't be around," I yelled at him.

I got up to walk away from him, honestly done with the conversation and him. However, I was quickly grabbed and pulled against a very hard chest. I was breathing hard at this point and I could feel his heart beating quickly through his chest as well.

"You can try to run all you want sweetheart, but I will always find a way back to you. If being across the world couldn't stop me from getting you, nothing will," he flipped me around so now our chests were touching and our faces were inches away from each other. "I understand you're not completely accustomed to my ways yet, but all you need to know for now is that you are mine and I am yours." His voice was filled with possessiveness and total seriousness.

I didn't know how I should be feeling, however, I was mostly just confused. Things were moving too quickly and I felt suffocated. Leo had everything figured out it seemed like and he left no room for discussion.

If he thought I was some girl that was just going to accept his terms and conditions, he was wrong. "Listen here Leo, I don't know anything about you and until that happens, we are nothing. You want us to be something, you need to ask me as a real gentleman would. I have standards." I patted his cheek with my hand, and he looked surprised, but that quickly changed to a look of challenge.

"You're a stubborn one huh? Good thing I like a challenge," he winked at me before letting go of me and going back inside.

He's gonna mess my life up.

Hope you guys enjoy this one. It's the longest one yet! Let me know what you think about it!

Chapter 7

The next day at school I was exhausted. I had a hard time trying to go to sleep because my mind just kept playing a repeat of what happened the day before over and over again.

I told my friends everything that happened and they all had the same reaction as me; they were all incredibly shocked. I suppose it's because none of us saw this happening since Leonardo literally never showed any kind of affection towards me before, and then boom, he's admitting his feelings towards me.

I hadn't seen Leo today at school which was a big relief because I needed some time away from him. It didn't help that he consumed my thoughts all day, but at least I didn't seem him physically.

I was sitting at our usual lunch table with Victoria and Claire when Elena came up to us out of breath. She threw her bag on the table and leaned over trying to catch her breath.

"What the hell happened to you?" Victoria asked Elena.

"I just saw," she took a pause to catch her breath, "Damon walk through the front doors," she took another pause, "with Leonardo." She finally sat down taking sips of water.

"Oh no," my eyes widened, I was really hoping that I wouldn't see him today.

"Yeah and he was heading the same direction that I was, which is here," she told me.

"Guys I've gotta get out of here, I don't wanna see him," I told them rushed.

"Why don't we just go to the library?" asked Claire.

"No, he would probably check there only after coming here, Aria's a nerd," Victoria said. I gave her a glare, "No offense Aria, keep up the great grades!"

"Great well where do we go then?" I asked the group.

"We could just stay here and Aria could face him," Elena suggested.

"No, that won't work, she's too awkward," Claire said with her hand on her chin as if she was thinking.

"Alright enough with the insults, I don't wanna see him so tick tock ladies. We have to think of something before he gets here." I told them looking panicked now.

"Let's just go to the bathroom, I mean he can't go in there," Victoria did have a point.

"Well, what are we waiting for, let's go!" I rushed them and we all quickly stood up grabbing our bags and speed walking out of the lunchroom.

We finally reached the bathroom and let out a sigh of relief. We were safe for now.

"We'll just stay in here until lunch is over which is in," Elena looked down at her watch, "seven minutes."

We all proceeded just checking our makeup and hair before a knock came at the door. We all looked stunned because who the hell knocks on the door of a public bathroom? The four of us looked at each other trying to decide who would open the door.

Finally, Claire threw open the door and standing in front of her was Damon. "What are you doing here?" She asked him with confusion in her eyes. That wasn't who I was expecting to see.

"I've been asked to get Aria," he said casually trying to look around Claire to see if I was in the room.

"Well she's not here, try again another time," Claire said closing the door.

The three of us looked at her stunned. She literally just closed the door on the future second in command of the mafia.

"Why did he come here looking for me?" I asked the girls.

"Oh my God, Leonardo found you," Elena whisper shouted.

"What do we do? We can't go out with Damon standing there," I whisper-shouted back. I did not ask for this much drama today.

Then another knock came.

"Who is it?" Claire asked the person on the other side of the door.

"Claire you know who it is, c'mon he needs to see her," Damon said from the other side.

A million thoughts swarmed my head. Why did he need to see me? How did he know I was in the bathroom? Why didn't he come to get me himself?

"I think I'm gonna throw up," Victoria said.

"You're telling me," I whisper shouted at her.

"Okay fine, you leave me no choice," Damon said behind the door and we all were silent trying to hear what he was saying. There was some shuffle behind the door and it sounded like he walked away.

I think at that moment we all let out the breath we were holding and I finally relaxed. We were about to walk out of the bathroom when the door opened.

It wasn't just a random girl that goes to our school, oh no it was much worse than that.

"Hello ladies, I need to have a moment alone with Aria," Leonardo greeted the girls, but his tone was anything but nice. He stalked into the bathroom with his eyes trained on me, but my gaze was on the girls, begging them not to leave me with him.

However, they paid no attention to my pleading gaze and quickly left the bathroom leaving Leo and I alone. Given how much I had seen Leo yesterday I didn't think that I would be this intimidated by him, but his face held a look of anger and challenge. I was scared of him at this moment.

"You're not supposed to be in here, this is the girl's bathroom," I told him, proud that my voice didn't waver much.

"Is that so?" He asked me almost mockingly, "who's gonna come in here and tell me I can't be with my girl?"

"Leo I'm not-" I began telling him but he quickly cut me off.

"Don't finish that sentence because it'll make me more upset than I am already," he told me and it quickly shut me up.

"Why did you hide away from me Aria?" he asked me with his head tilted waiting for my answer. He began walking closer to me, forcing me to walk backward to put some distance between us.

"I-I wasn't hiding."

"Oh really," he let out a low chuckle clearly picking up on my lying, but I didn't want to tell him the truth. "Why is it then that when Damon came to get you, your friend told him that you weren't in here?"

"I can't control her actions," I told him. This really was not the time to be a smart ass.

His eyes squinted at me, "Hm, but you do have control over your actions, and you could've come out of the bathroom. However, you didn't. Now, why is that?" He asked me, but it sounded more like he was demanding me.

"Because I didn't want to," I told him. I wasn't sure when I decided to be this brave, but here we are, poking the dragon with a stick.

Of course, this was also the moment that my back hit the wall of the stall behind me and he continued to advance towards me.

"Why is it that even though I told you last night that I will always find you, you still think you can hide from me? Hmm, tell me sweetheart," he said with his face a mere couple of inches from mine.

"Because I'm scared!" I exclaimed at him. I tried pushing him away from me but he didn't budge. "Everything is moving so quickly and I can't wrap my head around it. You quite literally slammed into my life and now I don't know what to do about it. We don't know each other Leo, you can't just call me 'your girl' and all these nicknames when I don't even know what your favorite color is!"

"Black."

"What?" I asked him confused.

"My favorite color is black," he said slightly amused.

"Oh my God, Leo I'm being serious," I told him very annoyed.

"This Friday I'm taking you out on our first official date and then you'll get to know whatever you want about me," his face was again a couple of inches away from mine and I wanted nothing more than for him to place his lips on mine. I think he felt the same way because his eyes kept flickering from my eyes to my lips.

We kept leaning closer and closer and I wanted, no needed to feel his lips on mine. I grabbed the collar of his shirt ready to push our lips together.

We were quickly pulled out of our moment when the bell outside rang signaling that class started.

I pushed him away from me slightly panting and I heard him groan.

"C'mon I'll walk you to class and get your tardy excused," he told me already grabbing my backpack and holding the door open.

"Thank you," I told him walking out of the bathroom.

In no time he resumed his spot walking next to me, "I'll be out of town from Wednesday until Friday, so make sure you don't get into any trouble while I'm gone." He seemed in a better mood than he was earlier.

"No promises," I told him smiling.

I could get used to him walking with me.

Chapter 8

The next couple of days were much more relaxed since Leo was out of town. I actually paid more attention to my classes and got the majority of my homework done so I wouldn't have much to do over the weekend.

Leo and I had been texting the past couple of days here and there. Through the messages, I learned more about him than previously which was an extreme improvement. I appreciated the fact that Leo understood that I wanted to get to know him better before our relationship moved further, and he seemed to enjoy getting to know me better as well.

I hated to admit it but I was beginning to miss him a little bit. I had really only been in contact with him for a couple of days, but he already had made such a big imprint in my life. I was starting to get a little crush on the future Mafia Don.

Today was Friday and I was currently on the way home from school with Elena, Claire, and Victoria. We were all going to my house so they could help me get ready for my date later.

My mom liked the idea that Leo and I were going on a date, and I could see the hesitation in my dad's eyes but he was okay with the idea after my mom talked to him.

For a while the girls and I sat around my room, gossiping and eating snacks before I realized that Leo was picking me up at 7 and it was already 5:30.

"Alright ladies, let's get started working on this mess," I told them gesturing to my now wrinkled school blouse and smudged mascara.

"Well first things first, you've gotta shower dude," Claire said pinching her nose in joking way.

"Ha ha you're so funny," I told her rolling my eyes.

Elena smirked, "Oh and make sure you shave."

My eyes widened at her comment and I threw a pillow off of my bed at her.

Victoria laughed, "Make sure you get everywhere." She winked at me, which earned her a pillow to her face as well.

"La la la not listening anymore you sickos," I said holding my fingers to my ears while walking into the bathroom.

I got into the shower and began to get nervous for the date. I had never been on one before so I didn't know what to expect. What do I do if it gets awkward? Where is he even taking me?

I shook the thoughts away and tried not to stress myself about it. I finished the shower and was now clean and hairless.

I put on my pink fluffy robe and kept my hair in the towel to dry. When I walked out of the bathroom, I saw clothes everywhere and the girls stressing over what I was going to wear tonight.

"I like these jeans with this jacket," Claire said to Victoria.

"No no no, what if he takes her something fancy, then she'll be underdressed," Elena said shaking her head at the outfit.

"We need to find an outfit that could fit either possibility," Victoria told both of them going back to my closet and flipping through the clothes I had.

I rolled my eyes at them and picked up my phone to text Leo asking how I should dress.

Leo :)

Hmm, you'd look good in anything, but the occasion is casual and dress warm ;)

I blushed slightly at his text, before turning back to my friends, "Leo said to dress casual but warm."

They all rushed over to the closet digging through the clothes, meanwhile, I walked over to my vanity to begin doing my makeup. I applied a full face of makeup with blush and contour. It was a date, I wanted to go all out for the occasion.

I took my hair out of the towel and grabbed my hair dryer to help make it dry quicker since we were now on a time crunch. It was nice and straight now, but I decided to go ahead and put it into a half up, half down style.

I was finished with all the beauty stuff while the girls were still working on finding me an outfit. I looked at the time on my phone seeing that it was around 6:40 now and Leo was going to be here at 7.

"Alright, ladies we gotta hurry this up because he's gonna be here in 20," I told them trying to hang up some of the clothes they had thrown onto the floor.

"Okay, we found your outfit!" Claire said walking out of the closet with Elena and Victoria.

They laid the outfit out on the bed and honestly I fell in love with it. It was a white knit, chunky sweater, blue mom jeans, and black booties with a little bit of a heel to add some height. Since it was freezing outside, I decided to layer it with a large, black fur coat. I put on some gold rings and a gold necklace with a crescent moon on it that my mom got me for my birthday a couple of years back.

I went into the bathroom to change and admired how I looked in the mirror. This outfit was definitely one that I would wear again in the future.

I walked out of the bathroom, "Okay ladies, how do I look?" I asked them posing.

There was a chorus of "you look so good" and "I love it" coming from the three of them.

"Thanks, ladies," I walked back over to my vanity to spray some of my Marc Jacobs perfume, "What time is it?" I asked them.

"It's 6:55," Victoria told me.

"Are you nervous Aria?" Elena asked me.

I sighed, "I kind of am, it's just people have always talked about how scary and mean he is, but he's acting like a completely different man with me. I'm scared that the rumors are true, that he is this monster who has no heart. I'm really starting to like him, but what if I end up regretting it?"

The girls all rushed over and hugged me. I guess I thought that I didn't really have anyone to talk to about these things, but I should've known that they would support me.

"Aria, people tend to just listen to the things that they hear from other people. I mean the majority of them haven't had an encounter with Leonardo before, they don't know him personally like you do. You can't let them dictate the way you feel about him," Claire expressed with a warm smile on her face.

Elena nodded, "Exactly like she said, keep in mind too that he's a future Mafia Don, he has to fit the role to the public. That's just how it is sometimes."

"Now you're gonna go on this date and have a fun time, then tell us all about it tomorrow at brunch," Victoria smiled at me.

"Thank you, I'm so happy to have you ladies in my life," we laughed at the unexpected sappy moment between us.

Then a knock came at the door, "Come in."

"Miss. Moon, Mr. Moretti is waiting for you downstairs," Mrs. Smith told me.

"Thank you, Mrs. Smith, I'll be down in a moment," I smiled at her.

I quickly gathered my purse with my phone, wallet, and gum and hugged all the girls before walking downstairs. They were gonna leave shortly after I did.

Once I finally reached the foyer my heart stopped. Leo stood there in black jeans, a black sweater, and black leather jacket, but he sure as hell looked good.

He looked like such a bad boy and I was digging not seeing him in his suit uniform like he was the last couple of times we hung out. I noticed him checking me out as well and I was happy to see that he liked my outfit choice too.

"Hey," he said almost breathless.

"Hi."

"Are you ready to go?" he asked me.

"Yeah let's go," I said smiling at him, before grabbing his hand and letting him lead me out the door.

I was excited to see what the night held for us.

I'm sorry for the lack of updates this week, I had my finals and was super busy! I'm officially out for the summer so get ready for some more frequent updates!

Chapter 9

We were in the car driving to the mystery location and neither of us had said anything yet. I guess we were both equally as nervous for this date.

I decided to start the conversation, "So where are you taking me?"

He turned to look at me, "It's a surprise."

I rolled my eyes. "Oh so you're not a big fan of surprises then?" he asked me.

"I guess not really if I know something is going to happen, I'd rather know the details than not," I told him.

"Interesting," he said nodding his head slowly as if he was absorbing the information.

"So, what do you like to do for fun?" I asked him trying to redirect the conversation.

"Spending time with you," he said smirking, "okay, really I enjoy reading whenever I do get a little bit of free time, but it rarely ever happens."

"Oh I love to read too," I told him excitedly. We had a common interest!

"What's your favorite book?" he asked me.

I thought about his question. I had read a lot of books in my life, so narrowing it down to one that was my favorite was a bit of a challenge.

"I think I would have to go with The Great Gatsby," I told him. "The ending is tragic, but I love the style, the glitz, and the glamour. Gatsby's and Daisy's love was so intense and I'd like to think that in another ending they were happy again, but I guess all good things do come to an end."

I noticed him just staring at me. "I'm sorry for blabbering," I told him embarrassed looking away from him.

His hand reached under my chin, "Don't hide away from me, I could listen to you talk about something you love all day."

My heart swooned at his comment, this boy was slowly winning my heart over.

"I actually haven't ever read The Great Gatsby," Leo told me.

My mouth dropped open at his comment, "You've never read-oh my God, Leo it's a classic. I'll have to let you borrow my copy sometime, you won't regret reading it!"

He let out a little laugh, "I would love that actually."

The car came to a stop and I looked outside the window. There was a huge ice rink with lights surrounding the area, and I could faintly hear music playing in the background.

"Oh my God, we're going ice skating?" I asked him with a huge smile on my face.

"We are indeed, I hope you like the idea," he said sounding a little nervous.

"I love it! I haven't been in so many years," I said with excitement in my voice. "I'm sure I'm a better skater than you," I jokingly said.

His eyes suddenly squinted, "Are you challenging me, sweetheart?"

My eyes widened and I was going to say no, but I was feeling bold today, "Yes I am."

"Challenge accepted sweetheart, what do I get if I win?" he asked.

"Whatever you want, same as if I win, I get whatever I want."

"Whatever I want?" he asked clarifying.

"Whatever you want," I confirmed.

"This challenge just got a lot more interesting sweetheart, you've got yourself a deal. I definitely intend on winning now," he smirked at me with challenge clear in his eyes.

The driver opened the door and Leo got out before I did, holding his hand out for me to grab like usual. I grabbed it and got out of the car. I thought he was going to let go of my hand, but he kept holding onto it, so I went along with it.

Leo and I walked to the entrance of the rink hand in hand, and I liked the way his hand felt in mine.

There wasn't anyone at the rink so it would just be the two of us which was nice. There were some guards standing by the entrance, and Leo nodded to them before telling them, "Make sure the grounds are safe, if anything at all happens, you tell me right away. Do you understand me?"

The men murmured a quick 'yes sir' before one of them pulled out a phone to give the orders to what I'm assuming were the other guards. I hadn't seen the Don side of Leo, but his tone was so serious and oozed power. The guards didn't dare to look Leo in the eye but instead kept their gaze nailed to the ground.

It surprised me, even more, when he turned back to me and his eyes went from emotionless to warm in a matter of seconds. How could his mood go from being that cold to warm so quickly?

"Let's go get our skates on," he told me with a smile on his face. I nodded my head and he led the way for us.

A table was set up off the side of the rink with snacks and sweets of all sorts. My mouth watered and I grabbed a chocolate covered strawberry and bit into it. Some of the juice slipped down my mouth to my chin, and I went to wipe it but Leo beat me to it. His thumb reached out and captured the juice before he placed his thumb on his mouth and sucked the juice off of it.

Suddenly it felt really warm, even though it was freezing around us. My heart was thumping in my chest and I felt my cheeks begin to become red. Leo's eyes held a look of hunger and he was so close to me that our chests were touching. At this moment I wanted nothing more than to feel his lips on mine.

Although the gesture felt purely innocent, I still couldn't shake off the intimacy the simple task held due to the closeness of the handsome boy in front of me.

However, our moment was quickly cut short when Leo cleared his throat, "How about we get our skates on?"

"Yeah," I whispered, "Let's do that."

He led me over to where the skates were by the bench next to the ice rink. I took a seat and began removing my booties, before attempting to put the ice skates on. As I was struggling to get the skates on, I felt Leo kneel in front of me, taking over to help me put them on.

"Oh it's okay Leo, I can get them on," I told him trying to remove his hands away from my skate.

He smirked on me, "Nonsense sweetheart."

His hand held onto my calf trying to help me guide my foot into the ice skate. My eyes widened realizing just how close Leo was to me, only this time it wasn't our faces that shared the closeness. He kept working on getting my skate on so I don't think he realized the fact that I had begun to freak out. I began squirming, trying my hardest to stay still.

This shouldn't be that big of a deal, but considering I had never been on a date with a boy before, I didn't know how to react to this type of closeness.

Soon enough he was finished putting both skates on my feet and I let out the breath I was holding. He already had his skates on so I grabbed his hand and we walked onto the rink together.

"Okay, so how are we going to determine who the better skater is?" I asked him trying to get an idea of what I needed to do to win.

He thought for a second then smirked, "How about whoever ends up falling first loses?"

My chances of falling were pretty high considering I haven't gone ice skating in so long, but as long as I remember to keep my knees bent, I should be good.

"Okay then, deal," I confirmed and we shook hands before actually getting on the ice.

My legs wobbled a little bit at first and I quickly grabbed on to the siding around the rink for support. I looked up and noticed Leo smirking at me before I narrowed my eyes on him and regained my composure.

"I'm fine, I just needed a minute to warm up," I told him rolling my eyes.

He smirked at me, "Sure you do sweetheart."

I started slowly moving on the ice and was quickly getting used to it, but then I looked up and saw Leo skating around the rink like an Olympic skater. My eyes widened, I didn't know he was this good at skating.

I started to get in the groove and was going around the rink in circles. I felt Leo pull up next to me and he grabbed my hand. We started to skate together and at that moment I felt content with life. He was able to make me forget any worries that I had at the moment and helped me just enjoy being in his presence. All doubts I had about being in a relationship with Leo went away as soon as I saw a genuine smile on his face instead of his usual smirk. It made me smile as well and I found myself growing stronger feelings for him.

At one point he helped me skate on one leg while holding my hands out in front of me for support. I was laughing and felt so carefree at the moment. Eventually, I began to grow tired and my legs were aching to sit down while Leo was still going at it like a champ.

I began to move towards the entrance of the rink, but my legs were fatigued from keeping them bent in a squatting position for so long that I straightened them out to relieve them of their pain. However, I felt my legs moving in front of my body and before I could grab onto the side to keep myself from falling, my butt was on the cold ice.

I looked up noticing that Leo had skated over to where I was and he extended his hands towards mine to help me up. His arms circled around my waist and he looked worried.

"Are you okay? Are you hurt anywhere?" He asked me, examining every inch of my body.

"Leo, I'm fine. It wasn't that bad of a fall," I eased his panicked mind.

He still didn't look sure, "Let's go sit down for a little bit."

I nodded and we walked back over to the table where all the sweets were before he kneeled down to help me out of the skates.

I took a sip of water to help ease my thirst after the workout that ice skating provided.

I noticed Leo looking at me so I met his gaze before he smirked, "Looks like I won the bet princess." I choked on the water that I was drinking.

Oh crap.

Chapter 10

The next day I was at brunch with the girls telling them everything that happened on my date the night before.

"He walked me to my door and we hugged and said goodnight," I told them taking a sip out of my strawberry lemonade.

"You guys didn't kiss or anything?" Claire asked me with confusion laced in her voice.

I shook my head, "As much as I wanted to, we didn't. Maybe he doesn't want to kiss me?" I began to get a little concerned.

"C'mon Aria it's not that, I mean it was your first date ever, you don't have to kiss on the first date," Victoria said.

"Yeah but all I'm saying was that there was a chance for him to get a kiss and he didn't take it, it's a little weird," Claire argued.

"Claire hush, it's not a bad thing to take it slow. Like Victoria said, it was literally their first date ever. I'm sure the next one will include a couple of smooches here and there," Elena said jokingly.

"Can we please talk about something other than Leo and I possibly kissing?" I asked them.

"Uh fine, does anyone have anything new coming up?" Claire asked the group.

Everyone thought for a second before Elena said, "Ooh I've got something. I don't know how I forgot to tell you guys about this but Justin is throwing a party next Friday and we were invited."

I thought about it for a second. Parties weren't really my scene and I was about to express my opinion before Claire beat me to it, "Oh we have to go! Ladies cancel any plans on Friday night because we are going to that party!"

Well, that defeats me trying to convince them not to go.

"Victoria, Aria what do you guys think?" Elena asked.

Victoria nodded, "We could stop by for a little bit."

"Aria?" Elena asked.

"Yeah, sure," I told them.

We all chatted a little bit more before we called the brunch good and decided to all head home. I got home and went straight to my bed, deciding to take a nap.

Most of my weekend consisted of taking naps and watching Netflix, but before I knew it, it was already Monday again. I walked into school feeling groggy and very underwhelmed. It was getting harder and harder to wake up and go to school every morning.

I walked over to the usual waiting spot where the rest of the girls were. I took off my coat and threw it into my locker before closing it and turning back to my friends.

"What's wrong with you Aria?" Victoria asked me.

I shook my head, "Nothing, just tired. What's going on with everyone else? Anything new?"

It was quiet for a moment before Elena spoke up, "I don't have anything. Looks like it's gonna be a boring day ladies."

We stood by the lockers for a little bit longer before deciding to walk to class. I guess it was going to be a boring day after all.

My second class of the day ended and I was walking out with Elena. We were chatting before I felt someone grab my wrist pulling me back.

I turned around expecting to see one of the girls or even Leo, but instead, I was met with a boy from my psychology class named Brandon.

"Hey Aria, you got a sec?" he asked me with a smirk on his face.

I looked over to Elena with a look of confusion on my face, and she shared the same look. I turned back to Brandon, "Uh yeah, I guess."

"Great, so I actually wanted to ask you if you would want to be my date to the party on Friday?" he asked me.

Did he not know about Leo and I seeing each other? Now I was going to have to be the one to break the news to him that Leo and I were going to the party together. I mean I guess Leo didn't actually ask me to go with him but it safe to assume that we were going together, right?

Before I let my thoughts drive me crazy, I began to answer Brandon, "Oh, you see Leo and I have kinda been seeing each-"

However, I was soon interrupted by a deep voice behind me.

"What the hell is going on here?" I whipped my head around and noticed Leo standing behind me looking like a beast ready to pounce on Brandon.

I looked at Elena and she looked just as shocked as I did. I turned back to Leo beginning to walk towards him.

"Leo hey-" I began but was cut off again.

"Aria, sweetheart, what is going on here?" He asked me in a sharp voice that I knew wasn't directed towards me, but it still sent shivers down my spine.

Before I could speak up Brandon spoke behind me, "I was asking her on a date, I didn't know she had a boyfriend. Keep her on a better leash next time man."

I turned towards Brandon, "Excuse me?" Who the hell did this kid think he was?

"What did you just say about her?" Leo asked. His voice was calm and deep but I knew he was anything but.

I saw Brandon open his eyes in the realization of the mistake he made.

Leo began walking towards Brandon with slow, mocking steps. "Why so quiet now, huh? You had a lot to say a couple of seconds ago. C'mon say it again, I dare you."

My heart was thumping in my chest and I was scared of what was going to happen next. I didn't know what to do, I was frozen in my spot.

Leo grabbed Brandon by his shirt collar and slammed him up against the lockers, causing the other lockers to shake at the sudden movement. He then threw a punch directly to Brandon's nose causing blood to gush out immediately.

"You dare speak like that about my girl? You dare grab her wrist forcing her into an uncomfortable position? You even dare to utter her name?" Leo was screaming in his face now. "Do you know who I am?" He asked Brandon.

Brandon nodded his head to Leo's question, "And you dare insult what is mine? You stupid, stupid boy. I think you owe her an apology."

Leo pushed Brandon down on his knees in front of me. I had tears coming down my face not recognizing the man in front of me and how different he was from the Leo on our date.

"Apologize to her!" Leo screamed at Brandon.

Brandon held his hands in front of him in a begging way, "I-I'm so sorry. Please for-forgive me."

"I forgive him, Leo let him go now," I begged Leo.

"No, I'm not done with him yet," Leo was looking at Brandon with a look of disgust on his face before motioning Damon over to him. I saw Leo whisper something in Damon's ear.

I was done with this game and honestly felt scared of Leo at the moment. I wiped my tears and grabbed Elena's hand pulling her away with me. We walked to the library before I sat down on one of the tables and broke down crying. I felt Elena's hand rubbing my back, and that one hand turned to three as I realized that Victoria and Claire were here as well. I wasn't sure when Elena had called them to meet us, but I was happy that she did.

When my crying finally seemed to stop I looked up at friends, no doubt looking like an absolute mess.

"Are you okay Aria?" Claire asked me in a gentle voice.

"I don't know honestly," I told them shaking my head.

"You can talk to us if you want, but we won't push you," Victoria told me putting a hand on my shoulder.

I took a deep breath, "That man down there, I don't know who that was. He was nothing like the Leo I had seen before, like the one from our date. I'm so scared though. I'm scared that the man down there is the real Leo. I mean, did you see him? Who knows what else he's going to do to that boy? I can't be with someone that violent. What happens the next time someone says something like that towards me? Do I have to deal with Leo forcing them into a submissive apology? Because unfortunately, I can't do that."

I was out of breath from my rant and my heart felt broken. The first boy I had begun to develop feelings for turned out to be a monster and I didn't know if I could accept that.

Before the girls could say anything to me, a knock was heard on the library doors and I froze.

"Can someone please check who it is? If it's Leo, do not let him in," I told them trying to wipe the mascara from under my eyes.

Elena went over to the door and opened it slightly, "Damon, she doesn't want to see him right now."

"Yeah well he needs to see her, c'mon Elena don't make this hard," Damon said. My breath hitched for a second knowing that Leo wanted to see me, but I quickly pushed those feelings away. I did not want to see him after the events that took place today.

I walked over to the door and threw it open, "Tell him that I do not want to see him and whatever was going on before between us, is officially over."

Before I could slam the door shut on his face, a foot stopped me from doing so. I was confused as to who it was but my confusion quickly turned to anger when I realized that it was Leo.

I rolled my eyes, "I don't want to see you, Leo. I'm assuming that you heard my message to Damon, so take the hint and leave."

I walked back over to where my stuff was, leaning down to grab my backpack, "Or better yet you can stay here and I'll leave." I began walking towards the door before his hand grabbed my arm stopping me from moving.

"Aria, please. I need to talk to you about what happened," He pleaded.

"Let me think about it," I put my chin in a mocking way as if I was actually thinking, "hmm no. Let go of my arm."

He quickly let go of my arm, "Please Aria, give me a chance to explain."

"No."

He groaned but began to get angry again, "I'm sorry but I can't apologize for what I did to that sorry excuse of a boy. He said things to you that he shouldn't have, hell things that no one should ever dare utter to you."

"Unfortunately Leo, people will say rude things in life. What're you gonna do, beat every single one of them up? Or do worse like the Mafia monster you've been trained to be?" I yelled at him.

I didn't realize, but at this point, all of the girls and Damon had left the room. I threw my backpack on the floor running my hands through my hair.

"If I have to I will, you are mine and no one will dare to speak ill of my girl," he said defending his actions.

I laughed at him, "You can't be serious Leo, you can't solve all of your problems or mine for that matter, by getting people to fear you. I can't be with someone that has violent tendencies like that."

He came closer to me, "I could never even think of hurting you sweetheart. Never you. You have to understand that I care too much about you to allow anyone to say anything remotely disrespectful towards you. Hell, there's not one person that's even worthy enough to say your name or even look in your direction for that matter. You are mine Aria. Pure and simple. I do not intend on letting you go now or ever."

"Leo I-"

"Let me finish sweetheart," he said, now very close to me. His voice was a mere whisper, but I heard every word he said, "I am a very protective man just like most of my family. With that being said, anyone who disrespects you or even makes you upset in the slightest will be dealt with. You can be unhappy with it, but at the end of the day, you are my queen. You are the only thing I care about and any problem you are faced with will be handled. I am yours just like you are mine, and I don't like anyone touching what's mine."

His lips crashed onto mine and I suddenly forgot about the earlier argument. I began to kiss him back and there was so much passion and fire that it scared me. How could he feel this way towards me even when we're this young?

His lips were soft and left me feeling addicted. My hands were wrapped in his hair and his hands found their way around my waist. It felt like we were kissing for hours when really it might've been a few minutes, but eventually I had to pull away to breathe.

We were both gasping for air and he leaned his forehead against mine.

"Does that mean I am forgiven?" he asked me playfully.

I smiled at him, "For now yes. I just need you to promise to keep the violence away from me Leo. I don't want to know about it."

"I promise sweetheart," he smiled at me, "I hope you'll consider being my date to the party this Friday?"

"It's a date."

I really did not know what I was getting myself into.

They finally kissed!! I hope you guys enjoyed this chapter because I enjoyed writing it. I also want to say thank you to everyone that's been supporting my story so far. All the love xxx

Chapter 11

Before this chapter begins I just wanted to mention that there is a slightly steamy scene. There is also mention of some mature things like alcohol and virginity. If it makes you uncomfortable I'm sorry, but they are all teenagers. However, it does not overpower the rest of the chapter. Enjoy your reading!

The night of the party had come and again the girls and I were at my house getting ready. The rest of the week, after the incident, had gone by rather quickly and I was happy it was the weekend again.

I was doing the final touch-ups on my pink lips followed by bold lashes, while Claire was helping Victoria with her hair and Elena was getting dressed in the bathroom.

I had my hair curled in waves flowing down my back. I was wearing my snakeskin mini skirt, a black sheer, long sleeved, shirt with a black crop top, bralette type thing underneath it. I paired it with black heels and to say I was serving looks was an understatement.

Claire had her hair straight and was wearing a red bodycon dress that hugged her figure very nicely. Victoria was wearing a red leather skirt and a black long sleeve, tight turtleneck with her hair waved. Elena wore a tight black mini dress with her hair in a high ponytail.

Considering that everyone would be at this party, we had to make sure that our outfits would be the center of attention for the night.

We headed out for the party. Leo had told me he had some business to take care of, so he was just gonna meet me at the party. I had one of my dad's drivers drop us off so we wouldn't have to worry about driving back home tired or anything.

When we got to the party, it seemed like everything was already in full swing. The music was loud and there were quite a lot of people on the lawn considering that it was freezing outside.

The four of us quickly walked inside, only to be greeted by bodies everywhere. However, space cleared in the center for us to walk through as soon as people saw us there. We went into the kitchen where the drinks and food were being held. There was all kinds of booze everywhere, but I opted out and decided to stick to my water for a little bit.

We were hanging out before Justin walked in with Vince beside him.

"Hey ladies," Justin said looking slightly intoxicated already.

I laughed, "Hey Justin, nice party."

"Thank you, Aria, and thank you ladies for showing up. Leonardo should be coming here shortly, but in the meantime help yourself to some drinks," he gestured to the large island covered in every kind of alcohol possible.

Claire smirked, "We'll keep that in mind, why don't you fix me up a drink Justin?"

Justin's eyes widened as did everyone else's. I knew that Claire thought Justin was cute, but I didn't know she was going to pursue him tonight.

"Lead the way, Claire," he said smirking at Claire. She looked at us with a huge smile on her face before grabbing Justin's hand and walking away with him.

I laughed quietly to myself before looking back at the other girls. However, Vince walked up to our group before interrupting, "Sorry ladies, but Victoria, would you like to dance?"

My mouth dropped open yet again, I didn't know that Vince had a crush on Victoria and by the look of shock on her face, she didn't either.

Victoria blushed, "Yeah, let's go." They walked away into the living room that had become the dance floor.

It was just me and Elena before she saw some friends she knew and went to say hi to them. I was standing alone, fixing myself a drink when I felt arms wrap around my waist.

I tensed for a moment before I smelt the familiar cologne that I grew to quite enjoy smelling.

"Don't you look absolutely ravishing tonight," his husky voice whispered in my ear. It sent shivers down my spine and I smiled before turning around in his arms.

"You look very good yourself," I complimented him.

His blue eyes stared straight into mine, "Not nearly as good as you, though I do wish I could have this sight all to myself and not every little thirsty boy in here," he slightly growled.

I rolled my eyes, but couldn't stop the blush that came across my cheeks at his comment.

"How was the thing you had to finish tonight?" I asked him taking a sip of my drink, completely comfortable with being trapped against the counter, in his arms.

He smirked, "We got it handled, it won't be bothering us anytime soon."

"Well, that's good," I smiled up at him.

"Let's go find a place to sit?" he asked me. I nodded my head and grabbed his hand before he led us to the living room where the rest of the gang was already. There was an open spot on the sofa next to Elena and some guy I had never seen before, but she seemed to be enjoying the company of, so Leo and I plopped down. Well it was more like Leo was sitting on the couch and I was sitting on his lap with my arm around his neck.

I blushed at our position, but I didn't make any efforts to move. It might've been the slight intoxication that I was under at the moment that was allowing me to show this much PDA in a social setting, but I was still enjoying it. On the slightly larger couch directly in front of the one we were sitting on, was Claire, Justin, Vince and Victoria, followed by another couch next to that one with Damon and a girl from my English class. I smiled at her and she smiled back at me.

I felt hands tighten around my waist and I leaned more into Leo, enjoying the way his warm body felt against mine.

"Guys we should totally play a game," Justin recommended taking another swing of his drink.

"Ooh, we should!" Claire agreed.

"Why don't we play truth or dare?" Elena asked the group.

Everyone agreed before Leo asked me, "What do you think sweetheart?"

I nodded my head, "Yeah let's do it."

"Great, why don't we do it in a spin the bottle type of way where the person who spins the bottle has to ask whoever the bottle lands on 'truth or dare'?" Justin asked us all, and again everyone agreed.

"I'll start off," Vince said finishing off the rest of his drink before putting the bottle in the middle of the table and spinning it.

The bottle landed on Elena, "Alright Elena, truth or dare?"

She thought for a second, "I'll choose dare."

Vince smirked, "Okay, I dare you to take three shots."

She scoffed, "Please, and here I thought you were going to make me do something challenging."

Vince rolled his eyes, before grabbing three shot cups from the table and filling them up with the clear liquid. She took them one by one, with the rest of us cheering her on.

When she was finished, she wiped the back of her mouth and smirked, "My turn."

She quickly grabbed the bottle and spun it before it landed on Damon, who looked surprised.

"Damon, truth or dare?" she asked him.

He looked like he didn't know which one to choose before finally deciding on, "Truth."

"Alright, are you a virgin?" she asked him.

I widened my eyes and looked at Leo who looked just as freaked out as I did. We turned to look back at Damon who surprisingly didn't seem that weirded out by the question.

"No," he answered.

I shook my head and took a sip of my drink trying to distract myself from the awkward question.

"Fair enough," Elena said leaning back in her seat.

Damon went on to spin the bottle, which landed on Victoria who was dared to send a foot pic to a random number. The spinning went on for a couple more rounds before it was time for Claire to spin the bottle.

The bottle landed on me and I rolled my eyes at the deviant look on Claire's face, "Okay Claire, let's get this over with."

"Okay Aria, truth or dare?" she asked me with a smirk on her face, causing me to get suspicious of what her intentions were.

I contemplated my options for a moment. If I picked truth she could ask me something very personal which could embarrass me in front of everyone, but if I picked dare she could make me do something just as embarrassing.

"I choose dare," I said trying to look confident in my answer.

Her smirk grew even more, but I ignored it and took a sip of my drink, "Alright Aria, I dare you to take Leo upstairs for ten minutes in heaven."

I nearly choked on my drink and I felt my cheeks begin to grow red. I narrowed my eyes at her, before standing up and straightening out my skirt.

I grabbed Leo's hand and pulled him up before looking back at the group, "Start the timer."

I led Leo up the stairs and I could hear the rest of the group let out 'oooh's' and other gross phrases, but I tried to block them out. The loud thumping in my ears from how hard my heart was pounding helped me out.

What were we going to do when we got to the room? I should've chosen truth or even had Claire change the dare, but instead, I let the confidence my drink offered me do all the talking and now I was back to my regular, awkward in these types of situations, self.

I walked to one of the doors and opened it, pulling Leo in with me. He was being strangely silent, but it was probably because he was just as nervous as I was.

I let go of his hand and walked to the bed, taking a seat.

"Listen we don't have to do anything, Claire can be very annoying at times. We can just sit here. I'm not even sure why I took her dare, but we can just hang out-"

I was cut off from my rambling by Leo sitting down on the bed next to me, placing his hands in mine, "Aria it's okay. It was a stupid dare, we can just hang out here before the time is up, we don't have to do anything you aren't comfortable with."

I sighed, "Thank you."

It was silent for a moment before I decided to speak up again, "If we were to do something I was comfortable with, would you be comfortable with it?"

He looked confused for a moment, "I guess it depends, what did you have in mind sweetheart?"

It had been a while since Leo and I had kissed and I honestly couldn't get his lips out of my head. The kiss was so passionate and amazing and I was wanting to experience it again. I suppose with the new found confidence I had developed through my drinks, now was my chance to get that moment again.

I took a deep breath before shuffling closer to Leo on the bed so our legs were touching. I looked him in the eye before reaching my hands out to grab the collar of his stripped button up shirt, noticing the couple of buttons he left undone at the top, and pulled his lips onto mine. It took him a second to wrap his head around what I had done before he began kissing me back. His hands gripped my waist and pulled me closer to him.This kiss was so much better than the last one we had shared and I was happy that I had made the move. I was also happy with Claire's dare, but I wouldn't dare tell her that.

I ran my fingers through his hair, gently tugging on the ends of it causing Leo to release a hum. I pulled away from the kiss for a moment, only to throw my leg around his waist so I was straddling him. He looked surprised for a second before I pulled his lips back onto mine.

He released a throaty groan and pulled my body even closer to his. I felt his black, denim jeans rubbing against my thighs. I never made out with anyone in my life, let alone with this much intensity, so I didn't know if I was doing it right. However, I don't think I was doing anything wrong because Leo seemed to be enjoying it just as much as I was.

I began to feel like I was losing air so I pulled away only for Leo to attack my neck with his lips. I let out a quiet moan and this encouraged him to continue his assault on my neck.

His lips met back up with mine before we were interrupted by a knock at the door.

Leo growled, "No way our 10 minutes are up yet."

"C'mon guys your time is up," I heard Claire say behind the door, "I hope you enjoyed it."

I rolled my eyes, hearing her comment. I was breathing heavily and was moving to get off of Leo before he grabbed my hips, stopping me from doing so.

"They can wait a little bit longer for our return," he said smirking at me.

I smiled back at him, quickly reconnecting our lips, enjoying being in each other's presence.

Third Person POV

As the two teens were completely wrapped up in each other, they didn't realize the looming threat soon making its way into their lives.

The man picked up his phone dialing a number before waiting for someone on the other line to answer, "Hello?"

"Boss," the secret man began, "It seems like the two are at some sort of party and you were right, he does have some sort of infatuation towards her."

The man on the other line took a breath, "I think it's time that we began our revenge."

The man hung up the phone before walking away from the house unnoticed.

"Enjoy the time you two have together, it won't be long," he muttered to himself laughing, before slipping off into the night.

I hope you guys enjoyed and there definitely are some things beginning to build up. Sorry for the long delay but I hope you guys enjoy!

Chapter 12

The next couple of weeks had flown by and it was the best couple of weeks of my life. Leo and I kept seeing each other and he kept treating me like an absolute princess. There was no drama at school with anyone, and the girls and I were still as close as ever. Life was working in my favor and I was enjoying every second of it.

This weekend was the launch of my mom's new clothing line and things had been busy around the house as she's been preparing for the fashion show. I was helping her out as well by being her unofficial assistant and creating some designs the past couple of weeks. This was also the weekend that Leo was going out of town, so I wanted to meet him at the airport to wish him safe travels.

I arrived at the airport and I was escorted by some of the workers to a more private area of the airport where the private jets were held. Of course, Leo would be using the private jet he was gifted from his father. I walked into the waiting lounge, past the guards that were outside the door and I automatically saw Leo sitting down.

I walked over to him with the biggest smile on my face. He noticed me almost immediately and his face went from completely emotionless to holding the biggest smirk ever.

I quickly jumped into his arms and he held me tightly. I was going to miss him, but I knew that he would be back in no time.

We soon pulled away and I felt my smile beginning to fall while tears filled in my eyes.

"Hey hey hey, what's wrong sweetheart?" he asked me wiping the tears from under my eyes away.

I sniffled, "I'm just going to miss you. How long will you be gone for?"

His smile didn't reach his eyes, "I'll be back before you know it."

Great, that meant that he had no idea when he would be back home.

"Why do you have to go to Italy anyway?" I asked him with a pout on my lips.

He sighed, "My father wants me to take care of the problems that are happening over there. All part of the training I suppose."

I smiled at him, "Well, make sure you do it quickly that way you can come back to me quickly."

"Will do il mio amore," he said pressing a soft kiss to my lips. It only lasted a second before I pulled away, remembering the present I had in my purse for him.

"Before I forget, I have something I want to give you," I told him reaching into my purse and taking out the book I had brought for him, "Remember when you told me you had never read The Great

Gatsby? Well, I just thought that maybe if you had some free time on the plane than you could read it or something. It's my copy so there are little notes I made in there if that's okay. I totally understand if you don't want to read it-"

I was cut off from my rambling with his finger against my lips, "Aria, sweetheart, I love this. I can't believe that you even remembered that conversation from so long ago. That means the world to me, you don't understand."

I smiled at him and pecked his lips, "I'm glad you like it."

"I actually got you something as well," he told me before reaching into his pant pocket and pulling out a long jewelry box.

"This necklace has been worn in my family for generations. My grandfather told me to give it to the girl that I knew I would want to be with for the rest of my life. This necklace I give to you as a promise. A promise of a future between the two of us," he confessed to me, opening the lid of the black box to reveal the most beautiful necklace I had ever seen.

It was on a gold chain with a ruby diamond in the center with an 'M' carved into the middle of the diamond.

"Oh Leo it's beautiful, I don't know what to say," I said breathlessly. This man practically just admitted to wanting to spend the rest of his life with me. I like Leo, a lot, and maybe I was even beginning to fall for him, but I didn't know what the future looked like. We're too young to determine anything that serious.

"You don't need to say anything, I just ask that you wear this necklace around your neck," his eyes shined possession and I mean there couldn't be any harm done to wearing a simple piece of jewelry.

"Okay," I whispered so low that I wouldn't be surprised if he couldn't hear me.

I turned around and held my hair up while he put the necklace around my neck. I felt weird knowing that he chose me to wear this family heirloom, but at the same time, I liked it. I liked that Leo did have genuine feelings for me and it put any insecurities I could possibly have, at bay.

I turned back around to meet his eyes that were shining with pride.

"When do you have to leave?" I asked him trying to change the subject.

"Whenever I want to," he smirked at me. I rolled my eyes and lightly slapped his chest.

"Hey remember that bet we made when we went ice skating?" he asked me with a look of amusement on his face.

I narrowed my eyes, "Yeah, what about it?"

"I never got to cash in my prize," he smirked at me.

"Oh yeah, what do you want?"

He thought for a second, "Hmm, I'll think about it. Though I will make sure that it's tasteful."

I was going to come up with a sarcastic reply before a knock on the door interrupted me.

"Come in," Leo barked out.

The door opened and in came one of the guards from outside, "Mr. Moretti and Miss. Moon, sorry to interrupt, but I did receive a message from Miss. Moon's driver that her mother expects her home soon to help prepare for the fashion show."

"She will be out shortly," Leo told the man in a cold tone.

The man quickly left the room and I turned back to Leo, "you could be a little bit nicer you know."

He smirked, "Only to you."

I rolled my eyes, "I guess I have to go now. Have safe travels and call me when you land."

I hugged him tightly not wanting to let go. I was never good at saying goodbye to people.

"I will sweetheart, be safe here. I'll still have my guards here looking after you and please don't fight me on this, it would give me peace of mind knowing that you are being kept safe while I'm not here to do it."

I sighed, "Fine, I'll miss you."

I quickly pushed my lips against his, wanting to remember what they feel like until the next time I get to see him.

He leaned his forehead against mine, "I'll miss you too baby," he whispered.

I walked out of the room holding onto the pendant hanging from my neck.

It was Saturday and I was preparing for the show with my mother. I was currently backstage and it was absolutely awful. People were running around, my mom was stressing out, the models were quickly trying to get ready, it was a lot to handle. The busy atmosphere of the show was keeping my mind occupied from Leo and how much I missed him.

He did call me when he landed and since then we had only been texting here and there. Nothing too much considering the both of us were extremely busy.

Finally, it was time for the show to begin and I went to go take a seat next to my parents in the audience as well as the rest of the girls and their mothers.

My mom's line consisted of florals and bright colors as we were entering the springtime now. I was happy to see that everything was going as planned and the audience was loving the new outfits as well. I was even making note of some of the pieces that I wanted to have in my closet because let's face it, you can never have too many clothes.

The show was wrapping up and it was time for my mom to walk out and thank everyone for coming to the show. She walked out and worked the runway like it was second nature to her before she began giving her speech.

"I wanted to thank everyone for coming tonight and everyone who helped make this show possible," she began saying.

I was trying to listen to her but my phone kept vibrating in my pocket. I was so tempted to pull it out and check who it was, but there was paparazzi everywhere and it would not be good for them to see me on my phone during my mom's speech.

I ignored the vibrating in my pocket and focused on my mom.

"I would like to say a special thank you to my daughter Aria, who has been such a big help in designing this line with me and will one day be taking over for me," she smiled at me before motioning for me to get on stage.

I stood up and walked the steps before meeting my mom in the center of the stage. There were flashes going off everywhere and I definitely was not used to all this attention.

I held my smile as my mom finished up her speech. We turned around and walked backstage. I hugged my mom and congratulated her on the success of the show. The girls and their mothers came back as well to congratulate her too. This night was definitely one that I will remember, and I couldn't wait to do this all in the future one day.

I was talking to all the girls when I felt my phone ring for what seemed like the millionth time tonight. I took my phone out of my pocket seeing that it was a number I didn't recognize.

I sighed, "Sorry ladies let me take this real quick."

I walked a couple of steps from the group before hitting the green button to answer the call.

"Hello-"

"Oh thank God Aria, I've been trying to reach you," her voice on the other line sounded rushed.

"Mrs. Moretti? What's wrong-" I was interrupted again.

"Aria something bad has happened. Steven and I are on the way to the airport right now."

My heart began beating very quickly and I gripped the pendant around my neck, "I don't understand wha-"

"It's Leo. He's been shot."

Hope you enjoyed this chapter! Thank you for all of the support!

Chapter 13

I don't remember the phone falling out of my hand onto the floor, I didn't hear it fall. In fact, it seemed as though I had become numb to everything around me. I had forgotten where I was for a moment before I turned around and noticed my best friends in the world, staring at me with confusion in their eyes.

I was also confused. It was as if I had forgotten what had happened, and everything had gone back to normal. Only that wasn't the case. The truth of the matter was that Leo had been shot.

As soon as my mind remembered that crucial piece of information again, it seemed as though everything in me shut down. I don't remember the painful sob that left me, or the moment that I collapsed to the ground, or when my friends and family ran over to comfort me. I do remember the pain I felt, the fear that was tearing through my soul.

A million thoughts were running through my head, and yet I could only focus on one. I had to go see him. I needed to be with him.

That was how I got to the moment I am now, on my way to Italy, flying on my dad's private jet. I was accompanied by both of my parents, who were going to show their support for the Moretti family. The girls, although they wanted to come along, couldn't due to school, but they were still texting me their support.

This flight felt neverending, but there was only an hour left before we landed. My mind was too preoccupied with worst-case scenarios to do anything but look out the airplane window the whole flight. By now, it was early morning, and I hadn't slept a blink all night. I didn't know what to expect, I had never been in this position before.

I was so scared. I kept thinking back to our last encounter and kept telling myself that it wasn't my last moment with Leo. I kept trying to convince myself that he was okay and just got skimmed on the arm by the bullet. Deep down, I knew that wasn't true. I knew that there was a possibility that maybe our moment at the airport would be the last time I ever get to see Leo, feel his warmth, feel his love.

Every time my mind went down that route, I had to force myself to think of more positive outcomes.

I noticed the seatbelt sign came on, but I didn't have to worry about it considering I hadn't moved from my position right by the window at all during the flight. I could feel the worried looks drilling into the side of my head by my parents, but they had no reason to be worried about me. I wasn't the one that was shot.

The necklace around my neck was the only thing that provided me comfort during the flight. I clung to it with every ounce of strength I had left in me. As long as I had the necklace, I had him.

———

The plane finally landed while my anxiety rose. I didn't know what to expect, especially when we finally got to the hospital, they took him to.

The bland furniture of the waiting room mixed with the smell of sanitation all made me sick to my stomach. My whole body felt like it was shaking and cold. My mom gave me one of my hoodies when we got off the plane, and I was thankful for the little warmth it offered me.

The women at the front desk led us to a private waiting room where Leo's parents were sitting and waiting. As soon as I saw them, my heart broke even more. Sofia's eyes were red and puffy, she looked like she hadn't gotten much sleep either. Steven was comforting his wife, but he looked worried as well.

"Sofia, Steven," My mom said softly to let them know we had arrived. Both of their heads snapped over to us before Sofia motioned for us to come into the room and sit.

I sat down across from Leo's parents while my parents rushed to the aid of Sofia and Steven. I didn't know what to do. I doubt there was anything I could do that would offer them any sort of comfort in this awful time of waiting.

"The doctors are still operating on him. He's been in there for so long, I just want to know what's happening to my son," Sofia cried in my mom's arms, "He was shot in the chest, who does that to a kid? He's just a boy."

Steven turned towards his wife, "I promise you that we will find whoever dared to lay a hand on my son, the heir of the Moretti name.

They made an awful mistake, and they will pay for this. I promise you."

I sat there, observing Don Moretti. The way he acted and talked, I could definitely tell where Leo got it from.

"David, would you come with me to go get some coffees?" Steven asked my dad.

"Sure, let's go."

They left the room, and I was sure that there were things Steven wanted to tell my dad without any of us hearing it. I was glad they decided to leave the room. I

let my eyes wander around the dull room before they landed on Sofia, who had a ghost smile on her eyes while looking at my neck.

I put my hand on the pendant trying to shield it from her in case she didn't agree with Leo's decision to give it to me.

"My son really loves you," she blurted out to me. My eyes widened, and I stared at her with confusion, "He told me about his feelings towards you so long ago, I was happy when he finally made a move on you. I was even happier when he told me he was going to give you the necklace his grandfather gifted to his grandmother. I always knew that you two would end up together, he was obsessed with you. Even when he was younger, anytime he saw you, he'd come home and tell me all about it."

She let out a small chuckle, "He would always tell me that he was going to get you, that he was going to make you his queen. The Moretti men, they love so deeply and strongly. When they love, they let that love consume every inch of both of your souls and if you haven't felt it yet, you will soon enough."

My mom looked deep in thought while I digested everything she said to me. I thought back to all of the moments I shared with Leo. He made me feel like the only person on the planet, and when I spoke, it was as if my words were the only thing that mattered to him. He cared about my protection and safety, my wellbeing, and happiness. He made me feel needed, he made me feel wanted.

Leo was possessive and wanted to make me his, just as I wanted him to be mine. He made me feel possessive of him. I realized that I wanted to make him feel like he mattered because he does. He is needed and wanted, I care about his safety and happiness. I care about him, but this was something stronger.

The feeling I got with him consumed me. We are young, the future is uncertain, but one thing I knew was that my feelings for this boy were strong, and it scared me.

A single tear fell down my cheek, "I think I love your son too."

My dad and Mr. Moretti walked back in, and I quickly wiped my tear away. They handed out the coffees, and my dad gave me my hot chocolate.

A moment of thinking in silence passed over us, everyone consumed by their own thoughts. A knock came at the door, and the doctor walked in.

"Don and Mrs. Moretti," he spoke with a thick Italian accent, "I have some news regarding your son. The bullet, although close to his heart, did not actually make it to his heart. He had a lot of bleeding, both externally and internally; however, we were able to remove the bullet from his chest, and he is now stabilized. They are taking him to the ICU where he will have 24-hour care while he begins waking from the surgery. You won't be able to see him for a couple of hours, so I would recommend going home and getting some sleep."

I let out the breath I was holding and felt a weight get lifted off of my shoulders. Leo was okay, he was alive.

"What a miracle that the bullet didn't hit his heart," Sofia said with extreme relief in her eyes while wiping the tears off her face.

"Actually, in the breast pocket of his coat jacket we found this book that seemed to slow down the bullet as it went through the book," he said holding up a copy of The Great Gatsby, "very lucky that he had this book in there."

My eyes were wide, and my mouth dropped to the floor. That was my book, the one I had given Leo before he left on this trip. The same book that had a bullet hole running through the middle of it.

Steven grabbed the book from the doctor's hand and opened it up to see my name written neatly on the inside cover page. He looked up at me, "Aria, this is your book."

I was pale, and I started to feel faint. What if I hadn't given Leo the book? What if he hadn't put it in his coat pocket? Would Leo still be with us?

Mrs. Moretti looked at me with tears in her eyes, "Aria, you saved my son's life."

I couldn't even process her comment before I passed out.

Hope you enjoy! Thank you for your support!

Chapter 14

I woke up feeling groggy and in a room covered in white. Where the hell was I?

My eyes felt sensitive, looking at the bright light in the room, and it forced me to keep them squinted. I looked around the room and noticed that my mom was sitting next to me, watching whatever was on TV.

"Mom," my voice sounded rough, and my throat felt dry.

Her eyes whipped over to me, and she stood up quickly making her way over to my bed, "Hey sweetie, how are you feeling?"

"I'm fine. Where are we?" I asked her not remembering the events from the last couple of hours.

"Oh, you don't remember? Ari honey we're here because of Leo, he's okay, and I think he might've woken up by now. They showed the book, and then you passed out, you've been out for the last couple of hours," she said, and everything came flowing back to me.

I tried getting out of the bed, "I have to go see him."

My mom held my shoulders down, "Let me call the doctor to make sure you're okay. I have some clothes so you can change and freshen up before you go."

I nodded my head and relaxed back onto the bed. The doctor came and told me I was good to go, but I needed to make sure I stayed hydrated, and I got enough rest. That wasn't going to happen until I saw Leo. I used the toothbrush and toothpaste the hospital offered in the little bathroom I had, connected to the room I was staying in. I changed into a pair of leggings and an oversized Gucci sweatshirt. My hair looked horrible, so I threw it up into a high ponytail.

I left the bathroom and met up with my mom, who was waiting for me, "Okay, let's go."

We walked to the elevator to go up to the 6th floor from the 2nd floor where I was staying. She led me to room '624', which was at the end of the hallway. Most of the rooms close to Leo's seemed to be empty, which gave a lot of privacy.

There were guards outside of Leo's door, and when they saw us, they let us in before quickly closing the door behind us. The security was strong, which made me happy.

I looked around the large room before my eyes met Sofia's tired ones, I offered her a small smile before my eyes were satisfied with the sight of Leo on the hospital bed. My breath hitched in my throat.

"He's sleeping now, he's been in and out all day. The doctor said that's normal and he should get as much rest as possible. He shouldn't be in much pain because of all the pain meds they gave him, but they still want to monitor it and make sure he's comfortable," Sofia said, rubbing her eyes.

"Sofia, you should go get some rest with Steven and David, you look exhausted. Aria can stay here while I take you to where they are," My mom told Sofia.

"Yeah maybe I should, just let me know if anything else happens," Sofia said, grabbing my mom's hand before they walked out the door.

"We'll be back, honey," My mom said, and I nodded my head in understanding.

I took the seat that Sofia was sitting in previously and looked at Leo. I was analyzing every inch of him while he slept, and I admired how peaceful he looked. I reached my hand out and began tracing the outlines of his face, from his eyebrows to his lips. He was perfection in every sense of the word.

I moved my hands away again and placed them on my lap. I didn't know what to do while he was resting, and while I understood that he needed to sleep, I wanted to make sure he was okay.

I decided to go on my phone and text all the girls what happened. They were all relieved to hear that Leo was alive, but they were worried about my well being. I assured them I was okay, and I passed out because I was overwhelmed by the past events. We texted a little bit more before I noticed that Leo had begun to stir in his bed as if he was waking up. Anxiety built in me, and I

had no idea why.

"Mom," he groaned out, his eyes still closed.

I stood up and walked over to his bed, "Leo, your mom went out for a little bit, it's Aria. Do you want me to call your mom or the doctor?"

His eyes shot open, and the faintest smile came on his face, "Aria baby, I didn't know you were here. You don't need to call them, I'm okay."

"Okay, how are you really feeling?" I asked him.

He laughed, but ended up wincing at the pain instead, "There's a slight pain but nothing I can't

handle."

I took a seat next to him on the bed and grabbed his hand, "Leo, I was so scared for you, when I heard what happened, I couldn't believe it." Tears began forming in my eyes, and I tried my hardest to blink them away.

A tear escaped and fell down my cheek, but he used his hand to wipe it, "I know baby, it pains me to think of what you had to go through. I promise you though that I will find the party responsible for this."

"I'm so happy that you're okay, Leo," I sniffled.

"You can't get rid of me that easily sweetheart," he said with a smirk on his face. It caused me to smile because only hours ago, I thought that I would never see that smirk again.

"Good, because I want you with me forever," I whispered to him, inching my face closer to his, "Are you in too much pain for me to kiss you right now?"

"Not at all, kiss me Aria," his permission was all I needed before I gently connected my lips to his, not wanting to cause him any pain.

We pulled away shortly afterward. I felt relieved, but I knew I would a million times better if the person that did this was found.

"Hey, baby?" he asked me.

"Hmm?"

"Did they tell you about the book?"

I took a deep breath and nodded my head.

"I read it, it's a pretty good book I must admit. I like the comments you made in it even more," he said, amused. I blushed remembering the comments that I made throughout the book from over the years.

"I told you that you'd enjoy the book. Actually, when they told me that the book slowed down the bullet, I passed out," I said laughing slightly trying to joke around.

Leo, however, didn't seem to enjoy the joke I was trying to make, "You passed out, and I'm only finding out about this now?" His eyes just grew angrier, forcing me to narrow my eyes at him.

"Leo, you are literally laying in the hospital with a bullet hole wound in your chest, and you're worried about me passing out? Unbelievable." I threw my hands up in frustration.

"Aria I care about your wellbeing over all else, if you are not okay, then I need to know about it. That is non-negotiable," he pressed in a cold tone.

I just rolled my eyes, "I wish for once you would be selfish with yourself and worry about the things regarding your health too."

"Unfortunately, that won't happen."

I sighed, "Look, I'm fine. The doctor said I'm all healthy and good, so you have nothing to worry about. Now knock that grumpy look off your face because my boyfriend just woke up from getting a bullet removed from his chest and I want to enjoy his company."

He reached for my hand again and held it, "I'm sorry sweetheart, you know that I get worried."

"You are forgiven because you are in the hospital, and I adore you," I leaned down and pressed a kiss on his nose, "now, what can I get you?"

"Some water would be nice," he told me.

"On it," I said, noticing a bottle of water sitting on the table next to the chair I was sitting at. I grabbed a straw that was also on the table and stuck it into the water. I walked back over and raised the straw to his lips for him to drink.

"Sweetheart, I can do it myself," he tried reaching for the water, slightly wincing at the movement.

"Nope, I am going to nurse you back to health. So you are going to accept me babying you for the next couple of days," I told him a matter of factly, and he took a sip of the water.

"As long as you're my nurse, I have no complaints. I actually have some ideas of things that you can do to help me heal quicker," he bit his lip, teasing me. It was the hottest thing I had ever seen in my life, and I had to take a second to compose myself and not do whatever he was thinking.

"Oh yeah, like what?" I asked him in a sultry voice, but before he could answer both of our parents walked into the room.

"Leo!" Sofia screamed, running up to her son and holding him tightly.

I tried getting up off the bed, but Leo's hand held onto mine tighter keeping me from moving.

"Mom," Leo groaned, "gentle, please."

"Oh, I'm sorry sweetie," Sofia apologized, backing away from the bed.

Steven also walked over to Leo and gave him a hug that was significantly lighter than Sofia's, "How are you feeling, son?"

"I'm feeling better, can't wait to get out of here and find the bastard responsible for putting me in here," Leo's voice changed to something that was venomous and dark sounding. It still blows my mind how quickly he can change his emotions.

"We're glad you're feeling better," my dad told Leo, and my mom nodded behind him in agreement.

"Thank you, I'm sorry that you guys had to make the trip out here on such short notice."

"Oh nonsense Leo, the Moon family will always support you. Plus Aria had to see you, she was such a wreck when she found out what happened," my mom confessed to Leo.

"Mom," I groaned, trying to hide my now red, blushing face.

Leo looked over at me with a smirk on his face, "I'm glad she's here."

"So any idea when he'll be able to go home?" I asked his parents trying to change the conversation and give my red face a break.

"We spoke to the doctor outside, he's considering having Leo stay in the hospital a couple more days that way they can slowly ease him off the stronger pain meds," Steven said.I nodded my head at this. That meant I would be staying here a couple more days as well because there was no way in hell that I was going to leave Leo. That would mean missing a lot of school, but I could always catch up on it on my own time.

"Aria, we'll be leaving tomorrow," my mom said.

Wait what?

"Mom, you can't be serious, we've been here for a couple of hours," I told her beginning to get angry.

"We have work to do, and you have school. Leo is fine here, and he will have his parents with him," she told me narrowing her eyes at me.

"I don't want to leave yet, mom, please," I begged her.

"We are not going to argue about this. We are leaving tomorrow, Aria," she said, ending the discussion.

I rolled my eyes, "Fine, but can I at least spend the night here with Leo?"

Before my mom could say anything, Sofia interrupted, "That is a great idea Aria, that way we can all get some sleep, and they can spend some alone time together."

I looked at my mom to see if she would argue against that, but she just sighed, "Fine, you can stay here tonight, and when we come back tomorrow we'll go straight on the plane."

They all eventually ended up leaving and it was just Leo and me again.

"I'm sorry my mom isn't letting me stay longer, she's been acting weird lately," I said, thinking back on her behavior. She had been acting strange ever since my conversation with Sofia. Maybe she wanted to put some space between Leo and me? It doesn't make sense, though because she was one of the people that was actively advocating for Leo and me to become a couple.

"Maybe she doesn't want you dating me. I mean we are in the hospital because I got shot. My life is already dangerous, and I'm not even the Don yet, I could see where she's coming from. She wants to keep you safe," he told me.

I sighed, "Shouldn't that be my choice, though. I don't care about your career choice, Leo, I care about you. I want to be with you."

His eyes lit up, and his smirk got even wider, "Good thing that I'm a selfish man because I wasn't planning on letting you go ever, baby."

I reached down and pecked his lips before pulling away, "You should try to get some sleep, the doctor said you need it."

"Okay, only if you sleep with me," he said casually; meanwhile, my eyes were wide, and my cheeks turned red.

"Leo what do you mean-"

"Aria, calm down, I meant sleep next to each other."

I sighed, "Oh, okay. We can do that."

The hospital bed was large, and Leo definitely was getting special treatment the time he had been here. There was more than enough space for the two of us to lay together.

He lifted the covers, and I slid in, making myself comfy beside him. He put one of his arms under my head and moved me closer to him.

"Is this comfortable for you? I don't want you to be in any kind of pain," I asked him trying to be as gentle as possible.

"This is perfect," he told me with his eyes closed already. I used the remote next to his bed to

dim the lights and make it more comfortable in the room.

"I've never laid in bed with a boy before," I confessed to him.

"Neither have I," he told me truthfully.

"Oh, you've never laid in bed with a boy before either?" I joked around with him.

He opened his eyes and narrowed them at me, "You know what I meant."

This only caused me to laugh, which eventually made him start laughing too, but only slightly since he couldn't do too much with his chest at the moment.

"I'm happy you're the first person I did this with," I said, closing my eyes and snuggling into his warmth more. His body was firm, and yet it was the most comfortable thing I had ever laid on in my life.

"I can't wait to be your first with many things, baby."

Then I went to sleep.

Hope you all enjoyed this chapter! Thank you to everyone leaving me comments and voting for the chapters! All the support means so much to me and I love you all!

Chapter 15

Sleeping next to Leo had to be one of the best nights of sleep I had ever had in my life. That was until the sounds of voices in the room got louder and louder, and someone was shaking me awake.

"What?" I groaned keeping my head lodged into the pillow. "Let me sleep."

I heard a deep chuckle, "Sweetheart, our parents are here."

My head shot up and I looked at both of our parents that were watching me in amusement. I wiped some of the drool on my off with the sleeve of my hoodie and cleared my throat.

"Good morning everyone," I said squinting my eyes at the bright light that my eyes weren't accustomed to yet.

"Good morning indeed Aria, did you sleep well?" Sofia asked me with a large smile on her face.

"I did thank you, now if you'll excuse me while I go crawl up in a corner and die of embarrassment," I told them all trying to get off the bed, but Leo held onto my hand not allowing me to. All the parents in the room laughed, clearing enjoying how uncomfortable I was by them seeing me lay next to their son.

"What time is it?" I asked Leo.

"It's about nine, how did you sleep baby?" he asked me, his thumb caressing the back of my hand.

I sighed, "Honestly, I slept amazing. How about you?"

"Best nights sleep I've ever gotten, I could get used to waking up with your snores and you sleeping on top of me," he smirked.

"I did neither of those things," I blushed and tried to defend myself. I do not snore, but maybe I did end up on top of him throughout the night. I couldn't help it, I guess I liked to cuddle.

He let out a small chuckle, "Oh sweetheart, you snore. It's cute though."

I just rolled my eyes, but I couldn't wipe off the smile I had on my face or stop the blush that continued to grow on my cheeks. I returned my attention back to our parents.

"Aria honey, we should be heading back soon," my mom had a sad smile on her face.

Any happiness I was feeling immediately left me and instead I was faced with the sad fact that I would have to leave Leo.

"Yeah, okay," I muttered, not sure if she even heard me.

"Can you all give Aria and I a minute alone to say goodbye?" Leo asked our parents.

Steven spoke up, "Sure, we'll be waiting outside."

They all left the room and I avoided eye contact with Leo at all costs. That was until I felt his hand under my chin, lifting my head so he could see my eyes.

"What's wrong little one?" He asked me. He had a frown on his face, and the moment a tear fell out of my eye, I saw a flash of anger in his.

"I don't want to leave you yet Leo. I was so scared only a day ago that you wouldn't make it, and now that you're here with me, I have to leave you again. It's not fair," I stated, my mouth quivering as I did so.

"Baby, listen to me. There will come a time in the future where we can be together with each other 24/7 if we want to. Until then, we have to work with what we have. I will come back home to you, I promise. I will be discharged from the hospital in two days and then I'll be spending another 2 days here in Italy in one of our houses to make sure that everything is okay. Then, I'll be on my way home to you where you can nurse me back to health all day, every day if you want to," he grinned at me, trying to brighten my mood, which it did because just seeing Leo's smile made me feel better.

"Okay, so four days. You better call and text me meanwhile," I said sternly, poking his chest.

"Of course baby," he pulled my arms into him so that we were hugging. I held on tightly, not wanting to let him go.

After many, many kisses and hugs with Leo, as well as saying goodbye to Steven and Sofia, I was walking out of the hospital with my parents.

The flight back to New York was quick considering that I slept through the whole thing, but it was already the next day which meant it was time for school.

There seemed to be an everyday routine when I was at school that consisted of meeting in the morning with the girls, going to my classes, meeting up with the girls for lunch, finishing my classes, then going home. Usually, there was homework afterward, but today there was a lot more considering that I had missed a day of school yesterday and my teachers hated me.

I was working out some problems I was given from chemistry when my phone rang. I didn't even look at who the caller was before I answered, assuming that it was one of the girls or my mom.

"Hello?"

"Hey, sweetheart," Leo's raspy voice answered on the other side of the phone. Butterflies immediately filled my stomach and a huge smile grew on my face.

"Hi Leo, what's going on?" I asked him, completely disregarding my homework and instead focusing my attention on my hot boyfriend who called me.

"Nothing much, thought I'd give you a call since you ordered me to call you every day until I come home," I could practically hear his smirk from over the phone, "what are you doing baby?"

I looked over at my homework, "nothing much, just laying on my bed. How are you feeling?"

He sighed, "A lot better, I'm sick of not being able to do anything. Just one more day and I get to leave this hell hole."

"I bet, hospitals suck. But hey when you leave that hell hole, you'll get to come to a second hell hole; school," I told him.

"Ha ha, don't remind me," he told me. I let out a little laugh, but I couldn't help it. Hearing his voice just boosted my mood.

"Italy is beautiful by the way. I would love to see it again one day."

"Next time you come here it won't be because I'm in the hospital," he told me.

"Well great, I would hope-"

"It'll be because we're on our honeymoon."

I froze, has he already thought about the chance of us getting married? We literally have only been dating for a couple of weeks. I decided to play this awkward moment off the best way I know how; by turning it into a joke.

"Not insinuating anything, but I don't want to go to Italy on my honeymoon," I added a little chuckle at the end to make it seem more like a joke.

"You're right, we should go somewhere we won't be spending every summer," he said thoughtfully.

If I had been drinking something at the moment, I definitely would've spit my drink out by now.

"What do you mean spending every summer in?"

He took a deep breath from the other side of the call, "Well, I was thinking that we should have a summer getaway with our kids, and I already have a house in Italy, but we can always buy another one if we need more space."

I felt like I was going to throw up. I really liked Leo, hell I admitted to his mom that I might be in love with him, but it sounded like our future was completely planned out by him already. I didn't know where my future stood, so I wasn't sure whether or not it involved being in Italy with Leo and our kids. However, I liked having options and control over my life, but now it seemed like Leo had completely taken over and planned out every aspect of our lives.

"Kids? Leo, how can you think that far into the future when we've been dating for such a short period of time?" I asked him.

"Aria, I've always known that we were going to be together for the rest of our lives. There's no one else I would want to be with for the rest of my life."

I was beginning to get frustrated and honestly a little bit suffocated, "Leo how do you know you want to be with me for the rest of your life? You've only ever dated me."

"Are you doubting the feelings I have for you Aria?" he began to sound a little bit angry.

"I'm not saying that I'm just trying to point out the fact that you seem so sure about us having a future together. I mean it seems like you have everything planned out already, I bet you've already picked out the colors for the nursery. For God's sake Leo, do I get any say in how I want my future to go!" At this point, I was yelling, but I felt scared and trapped. I had to push him away while there was still time to escape.

"Aria what are you talking about, of course you have a say. Is it bad for me to want a future with you? Do you not feel the same way?" He asked me frantically, adding more fuel to the fire of stress I was already under.

"I didn't say I don't want to be with you at all. I care about you Leo, but I don't know if I can see myself living in the life that you have created for the both of us!"

He groaned beginning to sound frustrated himself, "Aria it wasn't real, I was just saying what I imagined our future looking like. Is it a bad thing that I want to see us in the future with a family? Our lives can look however you want them to look Aria!"

I literally felt like I was going to throw up, "Stop turning this back on me, Leonardo! You know what? I need to go. I feel overwhelmed and I don't want to do this now. I need my space from you Leo, goodbye," I said my voice beginning to quiver now.

"Wait Aria-"

I quickly hung up the call. I ran my fingers through my hair and took a deep breath. Then the first tear came out, and then another one. Next thing I knew, I was sobbing.

The door opened, "Aria honey, I heard yelling- Oh my God," she ran over sitting next to me on the bed, "Aria, what happened?"

"I think I just broke up with Leo," I managed to get out through my sobs. As the words left my mouth, my heart broke even more.

"What happened between you two? You seemed so happy just the other day," she asked with worry in her voice.

I took some deep breaths to calm myself down, "We broke up because he started talking about our future. Mom, he had everything figured out. He was talking about kids and summer homes, I couldn't handle it. I don't know what my future holds, but it just felt like he was controlling our future together. I felt like I was suffocating. I've never even had a boyfriend before. Is it normal for a relationship to have so much commitment already?"

"Oh honey, it's okay to get freaked out with things like that. You're young, not many people think about their future, kids, or who they want to marry. You want to enjoy your youth, and I'm sure Leo wants to enjoy his as well. You have to understand too that Leo had to grow up a lot quicker than a lot of kids his age, including you. He's been getting groomed for his future ever since he was a young child, it's understandable that he thinks he has a clear picture of what his future is meant to look like. That doesn't mean it should pressure you, it just means that you both should have a talk about where this relationship is heading. Aria, you have to decide if you would like to be a part of his life or not, because I don't think that you'll have an out later on in life. You heard Sofia the other day, the Moretti men love strongly and deeply. Is that something you want?" my mom gave me a sympathetic smile.

I sighed, "I have a lot to think about mom, thank you for being here for me."

I hugged her tightly, missing the warmth she offered along with protection. She always knew just what to say.

"Anytime honey, you know that I'm here for you. Always," she kissed my forehead, before getting up and walking out the door.

I rested my head in my hands, as I thought about everything that was going on.

I finally made up my mind before realizing, I needed to talk to Leo.

I hope you guys all enjoyed! I hope everyone has been having a fun summer so far! What do you think is gonna happen between Aria and Leonardo.

Chapter 16

I had to talk to Leo, but I needed to do it face to face. Therefore, I had 3 days until he got home to prep myself for the conversation that we were going to be forced to have.

I put on my usual uniform before going downstairs to have some breakfast.

I saw my mom was still home which was surprising because she usually leaves before I even wake up in the morning.

"Good morning sweetie, how did you sleep?" she asked me while pouring herself some tea.

"I'm fine," I sat down at the table, "shouldn't you be at work right now?"

I began cutting into my waffle when she spoke, "Thought that I would have breakfast this morning with my daughter, everything at the office could wait."

I nodded my head, "Okay then, thanks."

"Mhmm," she was flipping through a magazine but I could feel her eyes glancing up at me every couple seconds.

"Is there anything you want to ask me, mom?" I asked her, slightly narrowing my eyes at her.

"Hmm what? Oh no. Just enjoying breakfast," She had a tight smile on her face. I slowly nodded before going back to eating my food.

A few minutes passed before she broke the silence again, "Actually there is something."

"Okay, what is it?" I asked her hesitantly.

"Have you thought about what you're going to do with the whole Leonardo and you situation?"

"Yes mom, I have."

"And," she carried out the 'n' gesturing with her hands for me to continue.

"And I have a couple of days to prepare and make sure my decision is final before I actually speak to him," I took a sip of my orange juice.

She shook her head, "Actually you don't."

"Don't what?"

"Have a couple of days."

"What do you mean? Why not?" I asked her, anxiety starting to build in my stomach.

"Yeah, um, he's actually on a plane back to New York as we speak," the words came out rushed, but I heard every single one of them.

"What?" I screamed, "He's not okay to leave the hospital yet! How is he coming back early?"

"I spoke to Sofia over the phone and she said that he got super angry over something, started threatening the doctors, forced them to allow him to leave early. Apparently, Sofia and Steven were at dinner when this all went down," She told me.

I gulped. I knew what he was angry about.

"When does his plane land?" I asked my voice in a whisper now.

"Around four, I think," she told me before putting a hand on mine, "And something tells me that this will be his first stop when he lands."

I groaned before letting my head fall onto the table.

After begging my mom to let me stay at home, she declined and forced me to go to school. So here I was, sitting at a lunch table with the girls.

I picked at my food, my anxiety not allowing me to have an appetite.

"Aria c'mon, try to eat something. Do you want to pass out again?" Claire asked me.

"I guess I wouldn't mind that," I shrugged my shoulders.

"Okay stop this grumpy, sad Aria. You knew you were going to have this conversation, only now it's today. Which is good because you can get it out of the way," Elena said shaking my shoulders.

"I'm scared you guys, he's not gonna like my answer."

"Well, he's gonna have to live with it no matter what. You made up your mind and he has to respect that. I mean you guys already broke up so this is the official goodbye," Victoria told me with a sympathetic look in her eyes.

"It's not that easy guys, I love him," I whispered, a tear falling out of my eye.

"Then why are you breaking up Aria? If you love him, why not be with him?" Claire asked me with a confused look on her face.

"Because I feel like we have two different visions of what we want our future to look like. Anyways everything is moving too quickly, I just need my space."

"Yeah right," Elena rolled her eyes, which caused me to narrow mine at her.

"Has he tried contacting you since yesterday?" Victoria asked me, probably trying to stop a potential fight from starting.

I shrugged, "I wouldn't know, I turned my phone off."

Elena groaned, "Aria, you can't avoid him forever."

"Don't you think I know that Elena?" I snapped at her.

"Listen, you can sit here and mope around, but you have to realize that you are about to lose a guy that is in love with you over something that won't affect you for like 20 years. You don't want space Aria, you're scared of what you feel for Leo. The fact that someone cares this much about you scares you because no one ever has before. You're willing to lose someone you really love, all because you're scared. Take a risk in your life," Elena snapped back at me, before standing up, "I think I'm gonna go to class early."

She left the table and I sat there thinking about everything she said. Elena was right, I was scared.

I got up and walked to class too, realizing that I wasn't so confident in ending things with Leo after all.

The ride home felt short and even though I took the longest time after school to get to the car, it still didn't delay getting home from school as much as I had hoped. I felt like I was going to be sick, but all I kept thinking to myself was what Elena told me. I had to be brave.

Taking a final deep breath, I got out of the car and walked towards my house. I noticed the increased amount of black SUV's and knew that he was already here. I went to reach for the door, but it opened before I could, with my mom on the other side.

"Hey honey, how was school?" she asked me, trying to sound positive.

"Where is he?"

The positive expression on her face fell, "He's waiting in the living room."

I nodded my head before stepping into the foyer, taking off my jacket and letting my backpack fall to the floor. I took a look at myself in the mirror next to the coat rack and mentally gave myself a pep talk before turning to walk into the living room.

I walked in and noticed all the security detail around the room, I resisted the urge to roll my eyes. I mean he was at my already guarded house, was it really that necessary?

My eyes finally landed on Leo who was sat in the middle of the room on one of the love seats directly in front of me. His eyes seemed angry, but I didn't let that break me down. I kept my head high, walking further into the room.

"Hello, Leo."

"Aria, I do believe there is something we have to discuss," His voice still held some warmth despite his emotionless face.

I nodded my head, "Are we going to get some privacy or are they going to hang around and listen?" I asked him motioning to all of the guards around the room.

He looked around for a second, "Let's go somewhere more private."

He stood up and I noticed him wincing while he did so. I quickly turned around, holding in my frustration over the fact that he was supposed to be in the hospital, but instead, his dramatic self had to come all the way to New York early to prove a point.

I walked across the hall to the room that was meant to be an extra study, but since both my parents already had ones in the house, my mom turned it into a little sitting room. The colors in the room were bright with yellows and blues; a complete contrast to the mood I was in at the moment.

I heard him close the door behind me, and I took a deep breath. Now was the time, so I turned around and faced him.

"Why did you leave the hospital early, despite your bad condition?" I asked him, my voice was at a normal level, but I knew that wouldn't last long.

He laughed but it wasn't a genuine one. This one sounded more mocking, and I didn't appreciate it.

"You're really asking me that, even though you tried breaking up with me over the phone yesterday?"

"What do you mean tried? I did break up with you," I told him confusion laced in my voice.

He shook his head, "No, we didn't break up. You're still dating me and it's going to continue that way."

I rolled my eyes, "Of course, here you go making all of the decisions for me, yet again."

"Are you seriously mad about me talking about our future together?" He asked me almost in disbelief.

"No, I'm mad at you because you just talk about spending the future with me like it's no big deal. We've been dating for a couple of weeks and you're speaking about marriage and kids. It makes me feel trapped like I have no way out," my voice began to rise towards the end.

"Sweetheart, I hate to be the one to say it, but there isn't a way out. You're mine, that's it," he spoke confidently.

I shook my head, "You can't say things like that and expect me to be okay with it. You can't leave me with the feeling of being trapped, and expect me to accept it."

He stalked closer to me, "I don't want you to feel trapped Aria. However, I picked you. You will be the woman I am with for the rest of my life."

I groaned out in frustration, "Leo we are 17 years old, things change. You can't tell me that we'll be together forever when we've only been together a couple of weeks."

"Stop bringing up how long we've been together. That doesn't matter. You know that we have a connection, a strong one at that. You know that you feel the same way towards me as I do towards you.

Why do you keep fighting it?" He kept walking closer to me, his voice rising and I knew that he was beginning to lose patience.

"Because I'm scared," my voice cracked. "I'm so young Leo, I wasn't intending on finding my future husband this early in my life, and I find it hard to believe that you were looking for your future wife this early on."

"I didn't need to look, she was always in front of me," his voice became softer, "baby, we don't have to rush anything and I'm sorry for bringing up the future this early on. I just get excited seeing the two of us together for the rest of our lives, and I can't wait for the day that we have our own family. However, I'm not planning on that happening anytime soon, I want us to enjoy our time together."

The weight I felt on my shoulders was lifted, and all of the fears I had before went away. I wanted to enjoy my life with Leo as well, without the stress of marriage and kids. I knew I overreacted but I'm a teenage girl with a full life in front of me, I want to enjoy my youth without worries and feeling trapped.

"I want to enjoy the two of us being together, without rushing into anything. I want to make the most out of the years we have together. I'm sorry for making a big mess out of nothing," I told him. At this point, he was directly in front of me and his hand reached out to cup my cheek. His large body covered mine, and I missed the comfort that he brought me.

"You're my girl, as long as I have you in my life I don't care what messes you make. Please Aria, don't ever doubt my feelings for you.

With all things uncertain out there, the one thing I am certain of is that I love you and I will continue to love you for the rest of my life."

His eyes were filled with so much passion, I almost couldn't handle starring into the endless, deep blues of them. There was one more question looming over my head that had to be addressed before we can officially put this fight behind us.

"How can you be so sure you'll be in love with me for the rest of your life?" I asked him.

"Because I just know."

"I love you too Leo."

And then he kissed me.

I hope you guys all enjoyed this chapter, and I want to say a huge thank you to everyone that has been supporting my book! It means so much to me, so from the bottom of my heart, thank you! :))

Chapter 17

Things in my life seemed to finally be looking up. Leo and I were happy as ever, basking in our love and each other. He was also recovering rapidly which I was happy about. He was finally back to doing his vigorous workout regime, which he was glad to get back into after claiming that he had lost all the muscle he had on him. I obviously didn't stop him, since I quite enjoyed seeing Leo all hot and sweaty.

Victoria and Vince had begun dating and were completely infatuated with each other, meanwhile, Claire and Justin were enjoying their off-again-on-again game. Elena had a secret boyfriend, and that was all we knew about him. She wasn't ready to tell any of us anything, and we respected her choice with that.

The SAT's had passed and I did really well on them, which was a huge relief considering I had never been more stressed in my life. Now there were only a couple weeks left of school, and I was more than ready to leave it.

On top of that, Leo's 18 birthday was coming up and I had no idea what to get him. Considering the fact that he was extremely rich and could afford to buy himself anything he desired, I wanted to get him something meaningful and from the heart. The only problem was that I had no idea what I wanted to give him. That is where brunch with the girls came in handy.

"What if you made him a picture frame and put a nice picture of the two of you in it?" Elena asked, trying to spark some creativity in me.

I shook my head, "He already has pictures of us all over his room."

"Oh I have something," Claire exclaimed, "What if you got him a new pair of shoes, you could never go wrong with a pair of shoes."

"Claire we're talking about Leonardo, not you," Victoria jokingly rolled her eyes causing Claire to stick out her tongue, "Aria he got you something pretty meaningful with the necklace he gave you, why don't you do something like that for him?"

I thought about it for a second, that's probably the best idea I've heard all of brunch, "You're right, the only problem is that I don't have a family heirloom to give him."

"You could go somewhere and design one, that would be even more meaningful because it's like it was designed for him," Elena suggested.

"I like that, well that takes one thing off my list of things I need to do," I thought for a second, "Hey you guys can still coming next weekend right?"

"Of course, plus Justin invited me so I have to make my grand appearance," Claire smirked.

"So you guys are back to being on-again?" Elena asked her.

"Yes, we are. I think we'll actually make it this time," Claire stated but seemed slightly hesitant. I really hope they would last longer than a couple of weeks because they actually did make a super cute couple.

We continued chatting before Victoria got up, "Oh, it's almost 11:30 I have to go meet Vince for some shopping," She smiled before quickly grabbing her bag and walking out.

The rest of us decided to leave soon after and Claire had gone to the bathroom, so Elena and I decided to wait for her outside. Things were okay between Elena and I, but I had never apologized or thanked her for basically being the person to snap me out of my over dramatic-ness and almost break up with Leo.

"Hey Elena, I never got to tell you this, but I'm really sorry for how I acted towards you during that whole 'wanting to end things with Leo and being a horrible friend that needed a reality check' phase. Thank you for telling me what I needed to hear," I offered her a smile.

"Thank you, but you knew I had already forgiven you. I'm happy that you didn't give up on someone that obviously makes you really happy," she told me honestly. I pulled her into a hug, thankful that I have such amazing friends in my life.

"Speaking of someone's that make us really happy, when will we get to meet the special man in your life?" I asked her, trying to get some deets on her secret man.

"Um, you know he's really busy and has a lot of things going on in his life and I'm not sure," she tried brushing it off, but I wasn't falling for her excuses.

I nodded my head slowly, "Right, well anyway, if he's available, tell him that he can come to Leo's party this weekend, so we can finally meet."

All she did was nod before Claire came out of the bathroom, "Alright let's go."

After brunch, I decided to go to a jeweler and have something designed for Leo. After telling my driver to stop at Cartier, I got out of the car and walked into the store. I was immediately greeted by tons of expensive jewelry.

I decided on getting Leo a ring, that way it was easier to wear and he would have no excuse to take off. A salesperson quickly made her way over to me.

"Hello, is there anything I could help you look for?" She asked me. She was dressed in all black and had her brown hair slicked back into a low bun.

"Yes actually, my boyfriend's birthday is this weekend and I wanted to get him a ring that matches the necklace he got me," I told her, and showed her the necklace that I had around my neck.

"That's beautiful, I'm not sure we have anything that would match that, but we do have some excellent rings you can browse through." She led me over to where the male rings were.

Immediately I saw one that I knew he would love. "Can I please take a look at this one?" I asked her pointing to the ring at the front of the enclosure.

She nodded and took it out of the casing before handing it to me. The ring was gorgeous, it was part of the "Leve" ring collection. It was a simple white gold band with little screw designs on the outside.

"That one is 18k gold and one of our more popular designs," she told me.

"Could I get something engraved on this?" I asked her, knowing exactly what I wanted the engraving to say.

"Of course, what did you have in mind?" she smiled at me.

After telling her the engraving I wanted and doing everything else that was needed, I was finally done and ready to go home. Now that I had Leo's gift picked out, the stress that was hanging over me was finally gone. I got back into the car and was resting my head against the window when my phone started to ring. I groaned before reaching into my purse and taking out my phone seeing that it was Leo calling me.

A smile immediately grew on my face and I quickly accepted the call putting it up to my ear, "Hey Leo."

"Hey, sweetheart what are you doing right now?" His deep voice asked me.

"I was driving home, why? What's up?"

"Can you come over, I need your opinion on some things for the party," I had been helping Leo plan out his party, and everything he did he ran it past me, despite me telling him that it was his party and he was the one in charge of making the decisions.

"Okay, I'll be there in like 15 minutes," I told him.

"See you soon baby. I love you."

I don't think I'll ever get used to hearing him say those words or telling him those same words back. "I love you too," I told him and then ended the call.

We were finally pulling up to Leo's mansion, and it was huge. The first time he took me here like a week ago, I thought he was playing a prank on me, but no it was his house. The house screamed luxury and had details that reminded me a lot of the houses I briefly saw while in Italy.

My driver opened the door for me and I was greeted by one of his workers. "Good afternoon Miss. Moon, would you like me to take your coat for you?"

I nodded my head, and quickly took off the coat I was wearing, handing it to him. The day was cooler than usual and yet I still had decided to wear a black and white plaid dress, with a black long sleeve turtleneck under it. I had stockings on underneath the outfit, but it still didn't do much to offer me warmth.

"He is in his study," the worker told me. I nodded my head again and told him a quick 'thank you' before making my way up the many, many steps of stairs I had to climb.

There seemed to be a lot more guards around here than usual which was slightly intimidating, however, I knew that they were just here for protection.

After climbing what felt like thousands of steps, my legs were burning but I finally made it to where his study was. I knocked on the door, before hearing a slight 'come in' and walking into the room and seeing Leo behind his desk on his laptop. He looked up and a huge smile met his face before he got up walking around to the other side of the desk to meet me.

"Hello sweetheart," he greeted me, pulling me into a tight hug.

"Hey baby," I told him, trying to spice things up by using nicknames too.

He pulled away and raised his brows, "I've never heard you call me anything but Leo. I really am starting to rub off on you."

"I can stop and go back to calling you just Leo," I told him.

He raised his arms in surrender, "I never said I didn't like it. Call me whatever you want, it all sounds good coming from your lips."

I rolled my eyes trying to ignore the sweet talking, but essentially I couldn't stop the blush that covered my cheeks. "What did you want me to look at?" I asked him trying to direct the conversation away.

He seemed to have noticed the effect his words had on me because his smirk just got bigger. "Oh yeah," he led me to the other side of the desk before sitting down on the chair and pulling me down to sit on his lap. He opened the tab on his laptop and showed me what he was looking at. "What do you think about this bow tie?"

I looked at him in disbelief, "You called me all the way over here to ask me about a bow tie?"

He shook his head, "It's not just a bow tie, it's the bow tie I will be wearing as I enter into adulthood. Now, what do you think?"

"Leo, it's a great bow tie. Is that all?" I asked him. He nodded his head at me.

"Yes, and now that we got that out of the way, we can spend some time together," he said cheekily.

I laughed and wrapped my arms around his neck, snuggling into him, "Okay. What do you suggest we do?"

He shrugged, "I could think of a couple of things." He leaned in closer to me and our lips were a mere couple inches apart before the door flew open and his father walked in.

I jumped off of Leo, completely humiliated while Leo looked completely cool. I'm seriously gonna start locking the door this is ridiculous.

Steven cleared his throat, "Hello Aria, good seeing you again."

I kept my eyes at the ground, too embarrassed to lift my head, "Good to see you too Don Moretti."

"Please Aria, we're practically family now, call me Steven," he said with a smile. I just nodded my head, indicating that I understood.

"Well, what's up dad?" Leo said trying to navigate the situation and find out the reason Steven barged in.

"Right, well we found a potential lead that might be able to lead us to who hired a hitman to kill you," Steven told us. My eyes widened, this was the farthest they had been able to get with this case in a while.

"So you think someone hired someone else to get a hit on me? The only people that would do that is anyone higher up," Leo was trying to make the best of connecting some dots, although he didn't have much to go off of.

Steven nodded his head, "Exactly my point, and given the fact that we have good relations with all other gangs, there are two that we could never be accepting of."

"The Russian and the Irish," I spoke out. I remember hearing about the feuds that had been going on between the three. However, while the Italian and the Irish did have bad blood for a while, the Russian feud was more recent.

Leo and Steven both looked at me with what looked like pride. "Well looks like we have some investigating to get to then. I mean it's not a for sure thing, but it's a lead that we definitely have to look into," Steven said.

Leo nodded his head, taking in all the information much like I was. I just wanted them to find the person responsible for shooting Leo, and I knew it was killing the whole Moretti family trying to find out who did it.

"Thank you for letting me know dad, I will definitely do some investigating on my own time as well," Leo told his dad.

"Of course, I will let the two of you get back to it," Steven smirked at us before walking out the door, closing it on the way out. Leo just laughed which earned him a slap on the chest from me.

I sat on top of Leo's desk, "I really hope you are able to find the person responsible."

"Me too sweetheart, until then let's go back to looking at bow ties because now I'm having second thoughts about the one I picked out," He joked with me, but it did the job of making me laugh and temporarily forget about the looming drama, waiting to unfold eventually.

Again, I hope you guys enjoyed reading this chapter. I do appreciate everyone voting and commenting on the story! Keep voting and letting me know what you thought about it!

Chapter 18

The day of the party had arrived and I had just gotten back to my house from picking up Leo's gift. I had to grab my dress and makeup for the party and then run over to Leo's to get ready. He hired a makeup and hair person for me which was unnecessary, but nonetheless, I was excited to get glammed up.

Walking into the house literally took my breath away. Leo had decided on the theme being 'A Night at Gatsby's with a Hollywood twist', which I absolutely loved and agreed to immediately. Leo wanted to dress as Gatbsy while I was his Daisy, minus all of the murder and betrayal at the end of the book and the whole 20's flapper idea.

His huge living room was covered in white fabric draped on the ceilings and walls to create a tent-like feel. There was a huge chandelier in the middle of the ceiling, with gold and black glitter everywhere. Tables were set up for dinner, and there was a dance floor to the side of them with a stage. The Moretti's definitely knew how to throw a party.

I saw Leo towards the kitchen, barking out orders, so I decided to go up to him. I laid my hand on his shoulder, "The party looks so amazing already."

He turned around to greet me, "I'm so glad you're here sweetheart, I was beginning to lose my mind." He sighed before giving me a peck and motioning one of his workers over to where we were standing, "Take her dress and bags up to my room."

The worker nodded before quickly grabbing the things from my arms. "Thank you," I called after the worker. I turned back to Leo, "Okay, you gotta stop stressing out, everything looks amazing."

"I'm not stressing, I just need everything to look perfect. There are some very important people coming over tonight and I need everything to go as planned," he rambled on.

"What do you mean? Who is coming over?" I asked him.

He hesitated, "Just some important people."

"Tell me," I ordered with my eyes narrowed.

"Remember that favor you owed me? When you lost at the ice rink?" he asked me.

"From a million years ago? Yeah I remember," I said not really sure where this was headed.

"Well, I'm cashing it in now, so I can't tell you," he told me.

I narrowed my eyes at him again, "Hmm fine, but you just gave up that favor for something stupid."

"I don't think so," he murmured more to himself than me. He gave me a tight smile and kissed my cheek, before grabbing my hand and leading me towards the kitchen. He sat us down at the table, "Now we're going to eat because I am very hungry and stressed."

I laughed slightly, as he motioned some of his workers to set out some food for us. However, I still couldn't figure out what Leo was hiding from me. I know that he cashed in that favor from the bet and technically he wasn't obligated to tell me anything, but my mind doesn't always think logically and I was still going to figure out what Leo wasn't telling me by the end of the night.

The meal wasn't that enjoyable considering that every five minutes Leo was yelling at one of the workers. Every time I scolded him for it, he completely ignored me and continued yelling. This was a completely different side of Leo; the one where he acts like a brat.

He had just finished yelling at a worker, who was near tears, and once she walked away I pinched Leo's arm.

"Why did you do that?" He asked me confused.

"Because bridezilla, you need to cool it with the temper. You've yelled at pretty much everyone here," I scolded him, "Now I am going to go shower because there are 4 hours left until the party and I need to start getting ready."

He sighed, "I'll come up with you and show you where everything is."

I nodded my head and we both walked up to his room. I grabbed some of my shower products from the overnight bag I had packed, before walking into the bathroom. I set them down in the huge, black marble shower.

"Leo, where are the towels? And can you bring me the pink robe from my bag?" I called out to him, feeling too lazy to go back out into the room myself.

He walked into the bathroom with my pink, silk robe in his hand. I grabbed the robe from him hanging it on one of the hooks on the side of the shower, meanwhile, he grabbed me a towel from one of the cabinets next to the toilet.

He handed the towel to me. "Thank you," I said, hanging it on another hook next to the robe. "I promise I won't take too long."

"Or we could shower together and take as long as we want," he smirked at me, walking closer to me.

I felt my face get warm, but I tried to play it off by rolling my eyes, "Ha ha, get out." I pushed him out of the bathroom, closing it on his face.

A smile remained on my face, but I ignored it, quickly undressing and getting into the shower.

I was in the middle of conditioning my hair when I heard the door open. This was alarming because Leo's shower doors were huge, see-through, and glass.

"Aria, can I come in? I have to shave," He called out from behind the door.

I panicked for a second, but I mean it was his bathroom and the doors were pretty fogged up so he wouldn't be able to see much anyways. "Okay," I told him, "just don't look."

"Okay," he said before walking into the bathroom, closing the door behind him, going towards the sink that was directly in front of the shower. "Damn woman, are you showering with fire? It's like a million degrees in here," he complained.

I rolled my eyes, "It's not that bad." I continued showering, now moving onto soaping my body.

I noticed Leo had started shaving his face, and his eyes were ever so slightly flickering over to the shower. I made sure to keep the front of my body towards the shower wall and not the shower doors, which was hard to do considering I now had to shave. I had shaved a couple of days ago so my legs weren't that hairy, but I just wanted to touch up on it.

I was finally done with my shower so I turned off the water and used my hands to get the excess water out of my hair. I opened the shower door and tried to reach for my towel, which was hard to navigate since I was still trying to keep the front of my body away from prying eyes. I finally gave up on trying to grab the towel like that, so I stepped half of my body out of the shower and quickly yanked the towel off the hook before retreating my full body back into the shower.

When I looked over at Leo, his eyes were wide. "Leo," I called out, "Did you see something?" For the sake of my embarrassment, I had to make sure I didn't accidentally flash him.

"Huh," he snapped out of his daze, "nope, nothing."

He went back to smirking, causing me to roll my eyes. I guess it wasn't that big of a deal if he saw something, I mean we have been dating for a couple of months now. Plus there was no way he could've seen anything extremely exposed. But then again, no one had ever seen my body like that before.

I dried off in the shower and wrapped the towel around my hair. Now I had to grab my robe.

"Leo? Can you grab my robe for me?" I asked him, not feeling like exposing my body a second time today.

"Yeah sure," I heard him say before he walked over and grabbed the robe from off the hook. I reached my hand out of the shower so that I could easily grab it, and when I felt him place the robe in my hand, I quickly snatched it back into the shower. I put the robe on and wrapped the belt around my waist tightly.

I stepped out of the shower and was greeted with cold air. I noticed that Leo wasn't in the bathroom anymore, so I decided to go back into the room and put on lotion.

He must've been in the closet when I got out because I didn't see him in the room. I pulled the lotion out of my bag and sat down on the bed, squirting some out on my hand and applying it to my legs.

Leo walked out of the closet with a change of clothes in his hands. "What are you doing?" He asked me.

"Putting on lotion," I said to him, "Are you gonna go shower now?"

"Hopefully, if there's any warm water left over," He joked around. I laughed sarcastically before going back to putting on lotion, moving up to my thigh. I noticed him staring at me.

"Is something wrong Leo?" I asked him.

"Nope, everything is fine," he said breathlessly.

I nodded my head slowly and continued putting lotion on. "Well, are you gonna go shower now?" I asked him while moving my robe higher up on my leg, that way I could moisturize the entirety of it.

I heard him groan slightly. "Yep," he said before he turned around and walked into the bathroom, "a nice cold one."

My eyes widened realizing what happened, but before I could dwell on it for too long, a knock came at the door. I got up, slightly confused at who could be at the door, and opened it when I noticed two women.

"Hi, Miss. Moon? I'm Mack and this is Isabell, we're the hair and makeup team," Mack said, her short red hair swaying while she talked.

"Yeah sure, c'mon in," I opened the door further to let them in. They had suitcases full of what I assumed was makeup and hair products.

Isabell pulled out a fold up makeup chair, much like the ones seen in Hollywood trailers, and set it up by the large window next to the bed. She gestured me towards the chair before they began doing their work.

Mack took my hair out of the towel, meanwhile, Isabell began applying moisturizer onto my skin. I noticed how bright blue Isabell's eyes were and how much that contrasted against her dark skin. "You have really pretty eyes," I complimented her.

"Thank you, but your eyes are much more beautiful Miss. Moon," she told me.

I smiled at her, "Please call me Aria."

"Okay before we go any further, do you want your hair up or down tonight?" Mack asked me, and I caught a slight southern accent laced in her voice.

I thought about it for a moment, "Down please."

She nodded and they both fell into concentration doing their work on me. I stayed on my phone, trying not to move much and stay out of their way.

Leo came out of the bathroom, now wearing a pair of sweats and a white t-shirt. I wasn't sure how Leo managed to look good in pretty much everything he wore, but the grey sweats looked extra good.

He came over to me while Mack and Isabell paused their movements for a second, "You already look so beautiful," he said kissing me on the lips causing me to blush. "I'm gonna run downstairs for a sec and then I'll be back up."

I nodded my head and he smirked at me, before turning around and walking out of the room. I noticed Mack and Isabell smiling at me causing me to blush even more. "He seems really in love with you," Mack said, meanwhile Isabell nodded in agreement.

"He is," I agreed with them, already aware of Leo's strong feelings towards me.

"What color is your dress?" Isabell asked me.

"Gold and black," I told her, thinking about my dress and how excited I was to wear it. The dress was beautiful and flattered my body so well. The minute I saw it in the store with Victoria, I knew that I had to buy it.

They worked on perfecting me for about another hour, and honestly, I was beginning to fall asleep. Who knew that getting all glammed up like this could be so boring?

I still didn't know what I looked like. Mack and Isabell thought it could be fun to surprise me at the end, but I was beginning to get antsy; wanting to see what I looked like.

The minute they put a mirror up to my face, I was in awe. My eyes were a gold glitter and black smokey eye, with a large winged eyeliner that made my eyes look more cat-like. My lashes were dramatic and thick, and my lips were coated with a little bit of gloss and a pink lip. My hair was in large, Hollywood inspired curls that were held with tons of hairspray. I knew this hair and makeup combo would look amazing with my dress.

I was thanking both Mack and Isabell before letting them out of the room, promising that if I ever needed my hair and makeup done again, they would be the first people I call. As soon as they left, the door opened and I was expecting to see Mack or Isabell at the door, thinking they might have left something, but instead I was greeted with Leo. A very handsome Leo with gelled back hair and his jaw on the floor.

"Aria, holy crap, you look absolutely breathtaking," he told me, taking my hand and twirling me around. "I don't even know what to say, I mean you're gorgeous every single moment of your life, but I've never seen you all glammed up like this. I'm so lucky to call you mine."

The blush on my face burned, and the smile I had was stretching my cheeks permanently. "You look handsome Leo, like a snack," I bit my lip.

"Baby, I'm just an appetizer, but you're the whole 5-course meal," he pulled me into his arms, and I couldn't stop the laugh that came out of my mouth, "God it's gonna be hard to keep my hands off of you tonight."

"Maybe I want your hands on me all night," I whispered to him.

"Good thing you're spending the night," he smirked and bit his lip, something that did things to me.

I let out an airy laugh, "Yeah in the guest room your mom said I could stay in."

He let out a low, deep chuckle and his eyes shined with hunger, "Baby, there's no way that your sleeping anywhere but in my bed next to me tonight."

My eyes widened at his response and suddenly I felt really hot. I tried putting some space in between us, but he seemed to disagree with my efforts and pulled me closer to him, wrapping his hands around my waist. I was breathless and there was a hunger inside of me I hadn't felt before, but I knew Leo could take care of. Before I could get ahead of myself I cleared my throat, hoping my words came out with confidence, "I have to get dressed for your party."

He glanced down at the watch strapped around his wrist, "Hmm, suppose I have to get dressed as well kitten. I guess we could always continue what we started later tonight." His head dipped down to my neck, his lips running over the smooth skin slightly before he moved his head back so we were face to face again.

All I could do was nod my head, not trusting myself to say anything out loud. He finally let go of me, of course not without his usual smirk, and walked over to his closet taking off his shirt as he did so. My God his body was fit, and my mouth was watering. I knew Leo was taunting me when he turned around and pretended to stretch, while my thirsty eyes took in every movement his six-pack made and he continued to smirk. He finally retreated back into the closet, and I let out a breath.

I was excited about the party before, but I was definitely more excited about it now.

Sorry for the long wait, this week has been so crazy for me! I want to also say thank you for almost 14k reads! That's insane but thank you to everyone voting and commenting and reading! Love you all and hope you enjoy this chapter.

Chapter 19

I admired my dress from the bag, too intimidated to actually take it out and wear it. It was by far the most beautiful dress I had ever had the privilege of wearing. The dress had a high neck and long sleeves, and fit tight like a glove. There was a beautiful gold design all over the dress on top of the black fabric that reminded me much of the prints seen throughout The Great Gatsby. The bottom of the dress by the knees flared out, and the back was open in a large oval. This was the dress of my dreams.

I unzipped the bag the dress came in and carefully slid the dress off of the hanger. I was left only in my underwear, deciding against a bra because I didn't want to ruin the open back of the dress. I stepped into the dress, sliding my arms into the sleeves, automatically feeling it cling to my skin. I did the little buttons on my neck, to secure the top of the dress, and I realized I looked damn good.

I wasn't one to be extremely insecure about my body, but there were days that I wished I could've had smaller thighs or a flatter stomach. However, this dress made me forget those insecurities and I embraced the body that I was given.

I took a couple of minutes admiring myself in the large mirror in the bathroom, before spritzing some of my favorite Marc Jacobs perfume and walking back into the bedroom. Leo was tying his bow tie in the mirror next to the closet before his eyes wandered over to where I was standing behind him. He turned around, coming to face me.

"So what do you think?" I asked him, giving a twirl so he could see the full thing.

He was quiet for a couple of seconds, and I was afraid that he hated the dress until he murmured a quiet, "Holy shit."

My smile widened and he walked closer to me, grabbing my hands, "I am at a loss for words, you are the most gorgeous woman my eyes have ever had the privilege of seeing. I don't know what to say, words can't even begin to describe how incredible you look right now. I am beyond blessed," he said breathlessly.

I felt my face grow hot before his hands grabbed my face, careful of the makeup and hair, "If only you knew the things you do to me, Aria." He smashed his lips against mine and I didn't even care about the lipstick that was surely bound to get a little messed up before I kissed him back. I kept my hands around his neck, not wanting to ruin his slicked back hair.

I pulled back from him, laughing slightly when I noticed that Leo had glossy pink lipstick now covering his lips. I used my thumbs to wipe it off. "I'm glad you like the dress," I told him.

"Oh, it's now one of my favorites," he said, giving me one last peck on the lips before moving back to finish tying the bow tie.

I smiled, moving over to the mirror and wiping some of the lipstick off that had made its way around my lips before applying a new layer of lipstick and gloss on top. I went over to the bed where my shoes were. They were black with a thicker heel and were much more comfortable than I was anticipating. I did the straps quickly before standing up.

I decided that I wanted to give Leo my gift before we actually went down to the party. I wanted this moment to be shared between the two of us, much like when he gave me the necklace, which was tucked safely under my dress tonight.

I walked over to my bag, grabbing the Cartier box that I hid in it, before moving back over to the bed and taking a seat. Leo was now putting on cologne so I decided to wait until he was done with that before calling him over. I admired how good he looked in his all-black tux, with the little gold, silk handkerchief sticking out from breast pocket. His loafers also had gold accenting on them, allowing our outfits to balance each other out nicely.

Leo turned towards me, "Are you ready to go?"

"Actually I wanted to give you something before we went down. Come sit," I patted the spot on the bed next to me, motioning him over.

"Baby, you didn't have to get me anything," he argued, walking closer to me. I rolled my eyes playfully, grabbing his arm and pulling him down to sit with me.

I took a deep breath before I started, "Not too long ago, you gave me the most beautiful necklace as a promise for a future between the two of us. I wanted to give you something that ties that promise between us as well." I pulled out the little box from behind my back, "Leo, this is my promise to you. I love you."

I opened the box and took the ring out. I grabbed his hand, "Do you accept this promise?"

"Aria, I am so in love with you, of course, I accept," he told me. I looked at his eyes and they held so much emotion and love. He had a real smile on his face, "this is the most thoughtful thing anyone has ever given me in my life."

I pecked him on the lips before looking back down at the ring, "I got something engraved on it."

"What does it say?" He asked me, but instead, I gave him the ring to look at it. He read it before looking back up at me, "I love you so much Aria."

"I love you too Leo," I kissed him again on the lips before pulling back, not wanting to mess up my lipstick again. I grabbed the ring from him and slid it onto his left-hand ring finger, knowing that the message 'Love you forever -A' would be a part of him for the rest of our lives.

Leo grabbed my hand before we began making our way out the bedroom door, and down to the living room where the party had already begun. With my hand in Leo's, we approached the big doors that separated us from the party.

He nodded at the guards, who opened the doors for us and we were immediately greeted by the beautiful setup. Now that the lights were dimmed, everything looked so elegant and truly like a scene straight out of a movie.

I was too busy admiring the decor that I almost didn't notice that all eyes fell on us, and there were a lot of them. I almost cowered down before I remembered how amazing I looked and how delicious the man standing beside me was. I had the future Mafia Don as my boyfriend, there was nothing I had to cower away from.

I looked over at Leo, who was already looking at me. I nodded my head, signaling to him that I was good to move on deeper into the crowd. We started walking and I kept my head up the whole time. For once I didn't feel like the awkward, stuttering Aria who hadn't even had her first kiss yet. I felt like a grown Aria; a powerful Aria with the world at my fingertips.

I saw my parents who looked to be in awe at my transformation, but I also saw a sense of pride in both of their eyes. I saw Leo's parents also had the same look of pride, but Sofia had a large smile on her face when she saw us. Most of the people in the room seemed shocked, other than my friends of course who had large smiles on their faces. It made me smile as well until I realized that we were going up on a stage and that was when this confidence act began to crumble.

I felt Leo give my hand a squeeze and I felt back at ease. I could do this, especially with him by my side. We climbed the stairs onto the stage where there was a microphone set up. Leo walked up to it, still not letting go of my hand. "Hello and thank you to everyone who was able to make it tonight. Tonight I turn 18, but until then we party," he cheered and so did the rest of the crowd. Then the party continued and Leo pulled me into his side, placing a kiss on my forehead. "Let's go say hi to some people," he told me, and I nodded before he pulled me along with him.

We went up to our parents first who were talking amongst themselves before Leo and I interrupted. Sofia was the first to notice us and she cleared her throat, "Aria your dress is absolutely stunning, you both looked so amazing together!" she gushed pulling me into a hug, before pulling Leo into one.

"Thank you, Mrs. Moretti," I smiled at her.

"Nonsense child, the love my son has for you makes you family. You can call me Sofia, permanently," she smiled at me and I blushed slightly. I nodded my head and smiled.

My mom was next to pull us into hugs, "You were like a true power couple up there. My daughter does have an eye for fashion."

I laughed at her comment before turning to greet my dad. "You look amazing sweetheart," he told me, placing a kiss on my forehead.

"Thanks, dad," I smiled giving him a tight hug. Leo then went to shake hands with my father hand while they talked a little bit. I swapped places with him so that I could greet Steven.

He pulled me into a hug to which I reciprocated. "You looked so natural up there Aria. I know you both will thrive having each other by your sides."

"Thank you, Don," he cleared his throat and I let out a little laugh catching myself, "Steven. It means a lot to me."

"I guess I have you to thank more, Aria. I'm guessing my son has told you all the details regarding me sending him to Italy two years ago. He used to hate me, he refused to speak to me. You somehow made him forgive me whether that was intentional or not, but you gave me my son back," Steven told me genuinely.

"Leo is very lucky to have a dad like you in his life. The exposure out there was probably very beneficial considering he will be taking over soon for you," I told Steven.

He looked at me shocked, "Oh so Leo did tell you about the announcement later tonight then?"

I looked at him in confusion, "What announcement?"

Before he could possibly explain himself Leo cut in, "If you don't mind dad, we're gonna go say hello to a couple more people before sitting to eat."

Steven smiled at us, "Of course, go ahead."

Leo pulled me away after we said goodbye to our parents for now, and yet I still couldn't stop thinking about what Steven meant by the announcement. What was going to happen tonight?

I soon saw the girls and I pulled Leo over with me to say hello to them.

"Whoa whoa whoa, look at that hottie coming this way," I heard Claire say when I approached them. I let out a little laugh and I noticed Leo smirk.

"I could say the same for you hot stuff, actually all of you," I told them adorning their amazing outfits. "Hey Justin and Vince," I greeted them, but I noticed there was a girl amongst the group that I hadn't seen before, "I'm sorry I don't think we've met before, I'm Aria and this is my boyfriend Leonardo."

"Hello, I'm Margot," She introduced herself to me. She had a tanned complexion and a beautiful accent. Her angular eyes were a deep brown, which complimented her dark hair very well. I noticed Elena grab her hand.

Elena cleared her throat, "She's actually my date, this is that secret lover I was telling you about."

It took me a minute for everything to click before I squealed going over to hug them both, "Oh my God Elena why didn't you tell us? Nevermind that, welcome to the group Margot."

I heard the others laughing but this was a huge shock to me, I don't know how I was oblivious to one of my best friends being gay. I let go of them and moved back to Leo who wrapped an arm around my waist pulling me closer to him.

"Sick ring Leonardo, is that the one that Aria got you?" Victoria asked Leo.

"It is, by far the second most precious thing in my life," he smirked, admiring the ring.

I narrowed my eyes at him, "What's the first?"

"You baby," he whispered, before placing a kiss to my lips.

I pulled away noticing all of our friends giving us suggestive looks. I felt a harsh blush come over my cheeks.

"We're gonna go talk to a couple more people, we'll see you guys in a bit," Leo excused us from the group, which I was thankful for.

After what seemed like endless hours of mingling with people I had never met before, my cheeks hurt from smiling and I was ready to eat. Leo and I were seated at the table with our parents, along with

Damon and his date. Her name was Crystal and she had dark auburn hair. She was super sweet as well and seemed to really like Damon.

They served the food and I tried to keep my elegance while eating, but it was hard to do considering I was starved and the food was delicious.

I was talking to Damon whilst Leo talked to his parents. "Are you enjoying the party so far?" Damon asked me.

I nodded my head taking a sip of my champagne, "Everything turned out amazing, aside from speaking to a bunch of people that I have never heard of."

Damon laughed before he turned more serious, "So what did you think when Leo told you about the announcement?"

There was another person going on about this announcement and yet I was still in the dark about it. I was going to have to pretend I knew what Damon was talking about and then maybe I could get it out of him.

"Yeah, I was quite shocked," I told him slowly, hoping I sounded convincing.

"Well that's completely understandable, I was completely surprised myself when I heard. I even think Leo was too, but I'm glad he has you by his side to support him," He had a warm smile on his face. I gave him a tight one back, I needed him to say more.

What could the announcement be that made Leo so surprised? I tried wracking my brain of anything I could've heard or Leo could've told me. Unfortunately, I couldn't connect anything to it.

I turned back over to Leo, tapping him on the shoulder. He turned around, smiling at me, "what's up sweetheart?"

I kept my tight smile, "Is there anything you wanted to tell me, babe?"

He tried playing it off as if he was confused, but I could tell that he knew I heard something. "No, I can't think of anything, though I do like the nickname you threw in there."

He had a chance to tell me and he didn't. I felt a little sting on my heart, I thought Leo and I didn't keep secrets. This secret was obviously something important if he had to use the favor I owed him as an excuse for him not to tell me anything.

Before I could explode and unleash all the thoughts that began mass producing in my head from over-thinking, I noticed Steven had gone up on stage. I saw Leo give Damon a look, and I assumed that this was the moment of the big announcement.

"Hello everyone, I want to say a massive thank you to everyone that was able to come tonight. My wife and I could not be more proud of the man our son has become. At just turning 18 in a couple of hours, he has become an intelligent, strong, powerful man that I know will do great things in his life," Steven boasted.

I was confused. This sounded like a normal parent who was proud of their child. Was this the big announcement?

"Leo, would you come up here for a second?" Steven motioned for Leo to come up on stage which he did, "I am so happy and honored to announce that when my son Leonardo turns 21, he will be taking over the position as the new Italian Mafia Don with the Moretti name!"

My eyes widened and my jaw dropped. What the hell?

Hope you guys enjoyed this one! Thank you seriously for all of the support, just last week I was talking about hitting 14k and now we're at 23k! That's insane! :)) keep voting and commenting, because some of the comments really have been making me laugh! love you all

Chapter 20

This chapter gets a little more spicey, but some things are revealed regarding some questions I've received ;)

I was taken out of my shock by the crowd, now standing and cheering around me. I slowly began to clap my hands as well, rising to my feet while still unsure of how to feel about this announcement. Twenty-one seemed a bit young for someone to take over something as serious as the mafia.

Leo came over to me with a huge smile on his face, and picked me up off the ground, hugging me tightly. I couldn't help the laugh that slipped my lips at seeing his excitement. He finally placed me back down on the ground and I placed my hands on his jacket, lightly gripping onto the collar of it.

"Baby, did you hear that! I'll be taking over at 21!" his smile was contagious and I couldn't help the huge smile that came over my face as well.

"I did hear, congrats love," I smirked before moving closer to his ear whispering in a sultry tone, "or should I say, Don."

I wasn't one to show tons of PDA, but after two glasses of champagne, I was ready to be all over Leo.

I pulled back, catching his eye while slightly biting my lip. His thumb reached out and released my lip. "God, if only none of these people were here right now baby," he groaned out.

My smirk widened before I leaned in, kissing him lightly on the lips. His arms around my waist tightened, but I pulled back from the kiss as quickly as it happened.

He looked confused, "Why did you pull away so quickly?"

"Because people are staring," I murmured.

"I don't care, you're mine," he narrowed his eyes.

This only made me laugh before I patted him on the chest, "We'll continue this later because there are people coming to congratulate you."

I pulled away from him, not before noticing the annoyed look on his face at the interruption. This made me smile even more, and the next hour was filled with people congratulating Leo.

My friends came over to me, while Leo was speaking to some people that were friends with his father.

"Hey Aria, I wasn't expecting that announcement to happen tonight," Victoria told me, taking a sip of her wine.

"Neither was I, but I'm happy for Leo. It's something he's wanted pretty much his whole life, I just feel like 21 is pretty young," I confessed to them.

"I remember my dad telling me that Don Moretti hadn't even become the leader until he was 26. I think Leonardo might be the youngest leader by far," Claire said.

I nodded my head, processing the information before Elena cut in, "Don't worry A, for knowing Leonardo for a short while, I've seen just how powerful he is. He can handle this, hell he could probably take over now if his dad let him. I mean, do you remember how terrified we were of him?"

I laughed slightly, thinking about the old days where Leo and I weren't together yet. Now, I couldn't even picture my life without Leo in it. The rest of the girls laughed, remembering how scared we were.

"Oh my God, we literally hid in the bathroom," Claire told the group, and I let out a loud laugh at that memory.

"It's so crazy to think about how much things have changed in the span of a couple of months," Victoria said.

"It is, but I'm happy they did," I said with a large smile on my face.

I felt a hand on my lower back. "Do you ladies mind if I steal Aria for this dance?" Leo asked.

"Go ahead, she's all yours," Elena smiled at the two of us, which caused me to smile as well. I was happy that my friends liked Leo. It was important to me that the most important people in my life got along well together.

I grabbed Leo's hand, while he pulled me to the center of the dance floor. It was a slow song, so Leo wrapped his arms around my waist, meanwhile, I wrapped mine around his neck. We swayed back and forth for a couple of minutes, enjoying the live music being performed and being in each other's hold.

I decided to break the silence. "Leo, why didn't you just tell me the big news yourself?" I asked him.

He shrugged, "I don't know, I just wanted to surprise you."

I nodded my head, "Well since you used the favor I owed you on something stupid like not telling me the big news, I decided to give it back."

He looked stunned for a second before smirking, "Why are you giving it back?"

"I guess I want to see what you could really do with it," I smirked at him, and he pulled me closer to him.

"Oh you will sweetheart," he said, pecking me on the lips.

I turned more serious again, "So, does this mean that once we finish high school you'll be working alongside your dad?"

"Pretty much, I'll be by his side, basically doing everything with him. My parents want to move to Italy once I take over so when I turn 21, I'll be on my own here," he said.

I opened my mouth to respond before he beat me to it, "How are you feeling about this Aria? I know this is a surprise, but I do intend on having you by my side the whole time."

I smiled at him, "I intend on being there and supporting you the whole way through. Hopefully by the time you take over, I'll be done with college and I'll begin interning with my mom."

He smiled at me, "Well I will be at every single show, front row watching my girl's designs walk down the runway."

I looked at the clock behind him, noticing that there were only five minutes until midnight. "Looks like in five minutes you'll officially be a grown man," I told him.

"I wouldn't want to take the next step into the adult world with anyone but you sweetheart," He told me, "Plus you'll be joining me soon enough anyway."

I sighed, "Only a couple more months."

"It'll come soon enough. I think being 17 was the best year of my life," he confessed to me.

"Why do you say that?" I asked him, wanting to know more.

"Because I got you," He smiled at me. "It's hard being in love with someone who isn't aware of the feelings you have for them. The moment you told me that you loved me, I knew I won at life. You are the best thing that has ever happened to me Aria, and I know that every year I get to spend with you, will be the best years of my life."

I couldn't help the tears that had formed in my eyes, "I love you Leonardo Moretti, more than you'll ever know."

His eyes held so much emotion and love in them, "I love you too sweetheart."

The clock hit midnight, and everyone shouted a loud "happy birthday". Leo and I were too caught up in our own moment to pay any attention to anyone around us.

"Happy birthday baby," I whispered to him, placing my lips on his. The kiss was deep and filled with love. I absolutely loved this man, and nothing was going to change that.

The night wrapped up shortly after and I was exhausted. My feet hurt and I was ready to take my makeup off. I said goodbye to my parents once everyone left before they did as well. Steven and Sofia had already gone to bed meanwhile Leo and I, along with the workers that were cleaning up, were the only people awake.

"Let's go upstairs?" Leo asked me. I nodded my head and we walked up the stairs together.

As soon as we got into the room, I plopped down on the bed to take off my heels. My feet were finally able to breathe. I got up to go to my bag and grabbed my pj's before walking into the bathroom. Leo was changing in the closet.

I took off the dress and slide it off of my body before grabbing the pink, silk cami top and putting it on. I then proceeded to put the matching shorts on as well. I usually wear a baggy tee and shorts to sleep, but I thought that I should wear something cuter given the occasion.

My beauty bag was already in the bathroom, so I grabbed a makeup wipe and began removing the hard work that was on my face. I washed my face with my cleanser and finished off with my moisturizer and eye cream. As tired as I was, there was no way I was going to go to bed with all that makeup on my face.

Feeling clean and ready for bed, I grabbed my dress that was now on a hanger and placed it back into the bag that it came in. I carried it into the room and laid it over one of the chairs. I noticed that Leo was laying in bed now, flipping through some channels on the tv.

I made my way over to the bed, pulling the covers up and sliding in. Leo's arms automatically pulled me closer to him, and I was snuggling him. We were laying there for a couple of minutes watching a movie on the TV, but I was just thinking about the night we had. I also began to remember the close moments Leo and I shared tonight, getting slightly hot thinking about them.

I tried shaking them out of my head, but all I wanted was to feel Leo's hands on my body and my lips on his.

"Are you okay?" Leo asked me, concern laced through his voice.

"Huh? Yeah, I'm fine," I told him. Yeah, Leo, I'm fine, I just want you to ravage me with your lips.

"You keep moving around, are you comfortable?" He asked me.

"Yep, all good here."

"Okay," he said unsure.

God his voice was so nice. I don't know what got into me, I was suddenly ready to jump his bones. I had never done anything remotely intimate with a boy before, and yet here I was, having all these thoughts about doing them with Leo. I wonder if Leo had ever done anything with anyone before. I mean he is handsome and I bet girls threw themselves at him all the time before we started dating. I felt a new feeling that I hadn't felt yet while dating Leo. Jealousy.

"Leo, can I ask you something?" "Yeah what is it, sweetheart?" He asked.

"Have you ever um," I took a moment to think about how I would phrase this question, "done anything with anyone before?"

"What do you mean?" he asked, confusion laced in his voice.

I sat up so that I was looking at him now. "Like have you ever done anything, sexual, with someone?"

He looked shocked at my question. "No," he responded to my question quickly, "never, you're the first girl I've ever been in a relationship with. You're the only girl I've ever thought about touching."

I nodded my head, happy with his response. "Why do you ask?" he asked me.

"No reason, I just wanted to know," I smiled at him, laying back down with my head on his chest.

That means I would be the first everything for Leo, which made me extremely happy. Every special moment we had together was even more special because we had only done them with each other.

I thought I would calm down after asking him that question, but it made me even hotter than before. Knowing that he had never been touched, made me want to touch him all that much more.

I began lightly tracing my fingers against his chest, which I know he enjoyed because he let out a small sigh. Screw it, I wanted him to kiss me.

"Leo, can I ask you something else?" I asked him.

"Of course baby," he responded.

I was quiet for a second, "Can I kiss you?"

I felt his heartbeat speed up. "Yes."

I sat back up, grabbing his face with my hands, before leaning in to kiss him. It started off as a slow kiss before his hands gripped my waist and I had one leg over his torso. I began running my hands through his hair, pulling him closer towards me to deepen the kiss. I felt Leo's hands grab onto my hips, before he lifted me, placing me on his lap. I was straddling him now, enjoying feeling Leo's hands run along my behind.

I pulled away from his lips, only to lean down to his neck before I began kissing along it. I heard him groan once I reached the spot under his jawline, licking that spot. Leo's grip on my behind tightened and I kissed up his neck, coming into contact with his lips again.

Leo quickly flipped us over so that he was on top now. I smirked into the kiss, loving that Leo was as hot and bothered as I was. He began kissing down my neck, down the valley between my breasts. I released a moan, enjoying his lips devour every inch of my skin.

I wrapped my legs around his waist, pulling him closer to the part that was desperately craving his touch. He hands wandered down around the sides of my stomach, and I pulled away laughing.

He had a grin on his face. "Sorry I'm ticklish," I admitted to him, seizing from my laughing.

"Good to know sweetheart," he said pulling me into one last kiss before lying down on the bed next to me.

I laughed, trying to catch my breath, "You're a good kisser you know that Leo?"

He wrapped his arms around my waist and pulled me closer to him, pressing a kiss on my forehead, "Practice really does help, huh?"

I laughed again, happy to be in the arms of the man I love.

Third Person POV

The man picked up the phone, dialing the number of his boss.

"What business do you have calling my number this late at night?" he boss angrily shouted at the man over the phone.

"His father made the announcement that he'll be taking over at 21," the man quickly told his boss.

He heard something crash in the background, almost as if it was thrown. He heard his boss's voice come back on the phone, "We'll have to take care of that now won't we."

I hope you guys enjoyed this one. The next couple of chapters might come a little bit slower because I've moved houses and I'm busy with unpacking, but that doesn't mean chapters won't be coming! Thank you all for the support, it means so much to me that so many of you are voting and commenting on my chapters! Keep letting me know what you think, love you all! :))))

Chapter 21

The next morning I woke up with a slight headache present; probably due to all the champagne I consumed the night before. The sun was hitting me directly in the eye through a little opening where the two curtains met, and I wanted nothing more than to get up and close it, but I couldn't find it in myself to do it. Plus, there was no way I would've been able to escape the arms that caged me against a very muscular chest.

I threw the bed sheets over my head in an attempt to try to get some more sleep, but I ran into another problem when Leo's snores practically screamed in my ear. I let out a groan and turned around so that I could see Leo's face. Normally I would have admired how handsome he was, but considering how tired I was, I wanted nothing more than to have the bed to myself.

I shook him slightly. "Leo," I whisper shouted, but he didn't move at all. I tried again. "Leo," I shook him a little more aggressively.

He let out a little groan and tightened his arms around me, yet he showed no signs of waking up. I huffed, getting frustrated but honestly I was too tired to try anything else so I sucked it up and laid my head on Leo's chest, trying to listen to his heartbeat instead of his snores.

I woke up a couple of hours later I was assuming, to find that Leo was still fast asleep. I, however, had a full bladder that I desperately needed to empty right away.

I began trying to pull Leo's arms apart that were still wrapped around my waist somehow, but this man was like steele, his arms were not budging.

I began shaking him with urgency, "Leo, you gotta let go, I gotta go to the bathroom."

This time it seemed like he was partially awake because he listened and loosened his arms around me, allowing me to rush into the bathroom. I did my business and decided to go ahead and brush my teeth while I was there. The headache was still slightly lingering, but with some pain medicine, it would be fine.

I decided to go back into the bedroom, noticing that Leo was awake and rubbing his eyes. Since I wasn't annoyed with him anymore, I took this as my chance to admire how cute he looked when he woke up. His dark hair was messy and his eyes were still slightly droopy from tiredness. He had a small pout on his lips, and I couldn't help but compare him to a child that just woke up.

I got back into the bed. "Good Morning sunshine, how did you sleep?" I asked him.

His arms wrapped around my waist and his he laid his head on my abdomen. "I slept amazing," he said but it was slightly muffled due to his position. "Please sleep next to me every night."

I let out a little laugh, "You like it because you get to cuddle me."

"Yeah you're right, but that's why you like it too," he said.

"Leo, you're a strong man with what feels like an above-normal body temp, it's like sleeping next to a sauna," I joked with him. "Oh, and add that you snore on there too."

He got up with a smirk on his face, "I'm sorry I'm so hot, baby. I can't help it."

I rolled my eyes, but couldn't help the smile on my face. "Oh, and I do not snore," he continued.

"Oh sweetheart, you snore," I smirked at him, remembering that it was the same thing he told me the first night we slept next to each other when he claimed that I snored.

He seemed to remember it too because he laughed a little, "Well then we're a couple that snores. Anyways, what did you want to do today?"

I shrugged, "I don't know, I'm fine with anything."

His hand grabbed mine, and I felt the cool metal of the ring on his finger against my warm skin, "How about we get some breakfast and go do some shopping?"

I nodded, "Sounds great."

He started to get out of bed but before he could I pulled his hand making him stop his actions. I pressed a kiss against his lips before pulling back, "Happy Birthday baby."

He smiled, tackling me onto the bed leaving kisses all over my face. I couldn't help the loud laughs that escaped my lips, but I knew that I could get used to mornings like this one.

Soon enough Leo and I were ready to go. I put my hair in an half-up, half-down style since it was still curly from the night before. My makeup remained minimal with concealer and mascara, however, I did decide to make my outfit cute. I wore a black, flowy skirt that went down to my mid-thigh, and an off-white long-sleeved turtle neck. The sleeves were slightly puffy, and the shirt was made of a mesh material, so I wore a black, cropped tank top underneath it. I paired it with my sneakers and my black purse. Moments like this made me happy that I was an over-packer, and packed five outfits for a sleepover.

Meanwhile, Leo wore black jeans, a white t-shirt, and a blue denim jacket. He definitely looked good.

We got to the breakfast place and it was a place I hadn't heard of before, but Leo swore that it was delicious. The place was packed with people since it was Sunday and brunch time. I noticed some students that went to our school there, along with some friends of my parents.

The hostess took us to a table that was more closed off and private from the rest of the restaurant, but that didn't stop all the looks that we were given as we walked by. The looks didn't seem to be judgy; they were more similar to those of admiration or awe. I suppose that the news from last night regarding Leo had already met most people's ears.

When we got to the table, Leo pulled out my chair for me and I sat down, giving him a smile.

Our waiter came over to the table shortly afterward, "Goodmorning, Mr. Moretti and Miss. Moon, could I start you off with something to drink?"

"Could I get lemon water and a strawberry lemonade please?" I gave him my order with a smile.

He nodded with a smile and wrote it down on his notepad, "And for you sir?"

Leo's facial expression was far from friendly, and I couldn't help but roll my eyes at his behavior. "I'll have a lemon water the same as my girl, and a black coffee."

The waiter nodded. "I'll have those drinks out right away," he said before walking away.

"You know it's okay to smile at other people Leo," I told him, amused.

"Yeah, but do other people know it's not okay for them to smile at you?" he asked me.

I rolled my eyes again, "People smile at other people to be nice Leo. It's something humans do to come off as welcoming."

"Why do you need to come off as welcoming? You have a boyfriend."

I began laughing, "Leo, are you jealous of our waiter?"

He rolled his eyes, "Of course not, that little boy is no competition to me."

"Right, okay," I said in a sarcastic tone.

His eyes narrowed at me, "Are you saying that that boy is my competition?"

I looked at him in confusion, "Of course not Leo, you're my boyfriend remember?"

He nodded slowly, "Just making sure."

I shook my head, before getting slightly out of my seat to press a kiss onto Leo's lips before sitting back down. "See, you're all mine."

The smile on his face grew, "Never doubted it for a second."

I laughed and soon after our waiter was back with our drinks. "What can I get the two of you to eat?" He asked us.

"Can I get the Belgium waffles with fruit on top and a side of hashbrowns?"

"Of course, the waffles are quite delicious," the waiter commented. "And for you sir?"

Leo's eyes were now narrowed at the waiter, despite the conversation we just had. "I want the eggs benedict with a side of bacon and hashbrowns."

"Right away sir, I'll have both of those out shortly." The waiter walked away again.

I took a sip of my strawberry lemonade, enjoying the sweetness on my tongue. Strawberry lemonade was one of my favorite drinks of all time.

"Mmm, Leo do you wanna try this?" I asked him.

He nodded, "Sure." He took a sip, and by the look on his face, he seemed to enjoy it. "It's good."

"I know right, strawberry lemonade is literally one of my favorite drinks ever," I said excitedly.

He smiled at me, "My favorite drink is either orange juice or black coffee."

I cringed, "I can agree with the orange juice, but the black coffee is blah. The taste is so bitter."

"What do you get when you go to a coffee shop?" He asked me.

"Anything fruity," I said matter-of-factly.

"Hmm, means you taste pretty sweet then huh?" He asked with a smirk, meanwhile, my eyes widened. I almost choked on my lemonade.

I composed myself, "I don't know how to reply so I am just going to act like that comment wasn't made."

He laughed, and I was glad he found this funny meanwhile my cheeks were burning. It wasn't so much in embarrassment as it was at the fact that I wanted Leo to find out just how sweet I was. These thoughts kept entering my head and I couldn't help them. But my boyfriend was hot, could you blame me?

"What's going through your head right now, sweetheart?" Leo asked me, clearly amused.

I shrugged, trying to shake off my thoughts, "Thinking about my waffle."

He just nodded, his smirk not fading. This might have something to do with the fact that I was ready to jump his bones last night, but I decided to go ahead and blame that on the champagne. I think I was at a point in time where I wanted to try things with Leo, but I just didn't know where he was at. I definitely wasn't going to pressure him into doing anything, but at the same time, I didn't know how to bring this conversation up to him. I'm not sure if any time was a perfect time, but I was sure that a Sunday brunch wasn't the best place either.

I was pulled out of my thoughts by Leo. "Any places you want to shop at?" he asked me.

I thought about it for a second, "I'm not really sure. I need some new skirts and dresses since it's getting warmer outside."

He nodded, "We'll just walk around then and if anything catches your eye, we'll check it out."

"Are you looking for anything today?" I asked him, hoping that I wasn't the only one with a shopping addiction in this relationship.

He shrugged, "Maybe some shoes or something, really if anything catches my eye."

I nodded, admiring how his right hand kept twisting the ring I gave him. "I like how that ring looks on your finger," I told him.

He gave me a smile, looking down at the ring himself, "I love this ring, it truly is the most meaningful thing anyone has ever given me."

I smiled at him. "I hope the next person to get a ring is you when I-" He paused for a moment, "I'm sorry, I forgot we're taking it slow."

My heart whelmed at his comment. I know I got freaked out by Leo talking about the future before, but now I know that my feelings for Leo are real and I want a future with Leo. Plus the plans we make wouldn't even take place for years.

"No Leo, it's okay. I love you and the next ring I wear on my left hand will be an engagement ring," I spoke with certainty in my voice.

Leo's smile got even bigger and it truly made my heart so happy. "Aria, I absolutely love you, and I can promise you that I will marry you one day."

He leaned over the table and pressed a kiss on my lips. I grabbed the collar of his shirt, not letting him pull away from me quite yet.

We were pulled out of our moment when I heard the waiter come back with plates of our food. His eyes were wide and he had a slight blush, probably embarrassed of what he saw. Meanwhile, Leo looked over the moon and as smug as ever. I let go of his collar, allowing him to sit back down in his seat.

The waiter placed my waffle and hash browns in front of me, and my mouth watered just looking at it. He placed Leo's food in front of him as well, and it looked delicious.

"Is there anything else I could get for the two of you?" The waiter asked the two of us. I shook my head 'no' while Leo actually replied "No."

"Right, well enjoy," the waiter said walking away.

I immediately dug into my food, drizzling the syrup over the waffle. I took my first bite of it and a small moan left my mouth. "Oh my God, Leo you were right, this place is amazing," I praised him.

"I told you, this could be our little breakfast place from now on," he told me, digging into his food. I just simply nodded, liking the idea of having a little place we go to regularly.

We continued eating, sharing stories and laughing. I loved spending quality time with Leo like this. Despite his reputation, I knew that Leo was genuinely a good person that loved with every fiber of his being. I was truly, madly, deeply in love with this man.

I know it's been a while, but life has been insane. I hope you guys enjoyed some sweet Laria (let me know if you can come up with a better ship name) content! Also, thank you so much for all the votes and the comments! I read every single one of them and a lot of them genuinely make me laugh so much so thanks for that! Also, let me know if any of you know someone who could make me a new cover for this book, I think this book deserves a more professional one!! Anyways thank you for the support, and I love you all !! :)

Chapter 22

Psa: if any of my readers make covers, or know someone who makes covers, please let me know. I really want a new one for this book! :)

We finished eating, and despite me trying to be polite and pay the tab, Leo ended up paying it. He said it was his "boyfriend duties" that he had to pay for the meal. I found it absurd and told him that one of these days I would pay for our meal.

Leo had his driver drop us off around 5th Avenue, where the majority of the nicer shops were located. The weather outside was gorgeous. It wasn't too hot, but it wasn't freezing either. This made me quite excited for the summer season that would be arriving soon enough.

Despite having guards trail us everywhere we went, I had an amazing time walking hand-in-hand with Leo down the streets of New York. We went into Bloomingdale's; one of my favorite stores. Immediately I saw tons of cute dresses that I needed to try on.

A saleswoman came over to help me, while I pointed out the dresses I liked and the sizes that I needed. Leo picked out a couple of dresses he wanted to see me in as well. The woman took us to the dressing room, where there was a nice seating area for Leo to sit and wait for me. Meanwhile, she led me into the changing room where I could try on the dresses.

The first one was a beautiful, champagne silk dress that hugged my curves like no other. The material was lightweight and the straps were very thin. The front of the dress towards the chest area swooped down giving a little bit of cleavage. It went to about mid-thigh and had little slits on the sides of the thighs. I was in love with this dress.

"Leo, are you ready to see the first one?" I asked him from behind the door.

"I'm ready when you are baby," I heard him say from the other side of the door. I smiled before taking one last look at myself and opened the door.

I walked out and noticed that his mouth was drawn wide open. "Holy shi-, I mean wow. You look absolutely amazing, holy sh*t."

I laughed and moved to gaze at myself in the big mirror by where he was sitting, doing a little twirl. "You think? I love how it fits," I told him, admiring my behind in the mirror.

"I love how it fits too. Sweetheart, add that one to the 'definitely purchasing' pile. Actually, you should probably add it into the 'wear for Leo when we're alone' pile," he said, his voice much huskier than before.

I could only blush and give him one last twirl in it before slipping back into the dressing room. I took the dress off, putting it back onto the hanger. I guess this one got Leo's approval.

The next dress was a light pink, ruffled, v-neck dress. The first thing I noticed when I put it on was the plunging neckline and the cleavage that was spilling from it. I mean it didn't look bad, but it definitely was out of my comfort zone. The rest of the dress was absolutely amazing, however. The bottom wasn't tight-fitting, but it was still flattering and made my waist look snatched.

"Leo, I don't know how I feel about this one," I told him, trying to find a way to make my cleavage fit into it more modestly.

"Come out and show me," I heard him say. I took a breath. At least he would be honest about whether he liked it or not.

I opened the door, keeping my hand on my chest to cover up some of the extreme cleavage.

"Aria, why is your hand there?" he asked me, looking slightly confused.

"Because it's a bit... much," I told him honestly.

"It's probably not that bad, let me see," he told me.

I nodded, sighing, before taking my hand off of my chest noticing right away how his eyes widened. His eyes stayed glued to my chest.

"Do you think it's a bit much?" I asked him, trying to snap him out of this trance.

"Hmm what," he blinked a couple of times, "Oh no, it's not too much. The dress is stunning, fits amazing." His eyes remained on my chest and I rolled my eyes. I decided to play with him a little bit.

I walked closer to him, leaning over him so that my chest was in front of his gaze, "Oh you should feel the material, it's very soft." My voice turned more sultry and I noticed him gulp.

"Oh no, I believe you. I'm sure it is-" he began, but I cut him off.

I grabbed his hand placing it on the ruffle part of the dress that was a couple of inches away from my breast. "See, it's soft right?" I was truly baffled at how much of an effect some fat on my chest had on him.

He cleared his throat, "Yep, it's soft alright."

I pulled away from him, slapping him lightly on the chest. "Hope you enjoyed that show," I said sarcastically, walking back into the fitting room.

"You know I did," he called out to me. "Oh and add that one to the 'definitely purchasing pile'."

I could practically hear the smirk on his face, and I rolled my eyes. I looked at myself in the mirror, enjoying the way that I looked while also cursing myself for the blush on my cheeks.

After what seemed like hours of me trying on different dresses and getting Leo's opinion on each of them, we were ready to purchase the ten dresses that made the cut.

The saleswoman gave me the total, and holy crap it was definitely going to dent my bank account. I pulled out my card to pay, but Leo simply pushed the card away and handed the woman his card.

I looked at him in shock, because that wasn't just brunch, that was thousands of dollars. "Leo, why did you do that? I would have paid for it myself," I told him, trying to figure out why he paid.

"Nonsense, I told you that I would pay for you. It's my boyfriend duty," he tried brushing me off, but he should know by now that I am way too stubborn for that.

"Leo, you said you'd pay for our meals together, not my thousands of dollars shopping tab," I tried to explain to him as we began walking out of the store.

He shrugged, "Well then you could go ahead and add paying for your shopping tab, to the list."

My mouth was open in shock, "Leo at least let me pay you back for it, it was a lot of money."

He stopped walking and turned towards me, placing his hands on my cheeks. "Aria, baby, I have more than enough money to last me multiple lifetimes and I haven't even inherited the business yet. Believe me, baby, your tab did nothing to my bank account. And I am more than happy to buy you anything that your little heart desires." He kissed me on the forehead and grabbed me by the hand continuing to walk down the street.

I, however, couldn't just get over his little confession. How much money did Leo have? What does one do with that kind of money? I felt bad for using his money like that. I mean it wasn't like I was using him for money, considering I had my own, but I still felt weird about using it.

I stopped my thoughts, not allowing them to make me lose my mind. Instead, I focused on the slight breeze that felt nice flowing through my hair. It was less nice, however, when I caught whiff of the gross smelling sidewalks that inhabit New York.

The sun was starting to set at this point, and it made me upset to think that the day was almost over. I loved spending time with Leo.

We were walking past the last alleyway, trying to make it up the street where the driver was waiting for us. I felt my phone vibrate in my bag, and I stopped for a second to reach into my purse to retrieve it. My phone was soon tumbling out of my hands when I felt something pull me back. I assumed that my skirt got caught on something, but when I felt arms around my waist only to notice that Leo was a couple of steps ahead of me, I knew something was wrong. I let out a scream before I felt a dirty hand slap against my mouth, silencing me.

Leo turned around at hearing my scream. His face was shocked, and then a look of anger emerged. Meanwhile, I was gagging on the disgusting hand that was suffocating me with its stench.

"Let go of her. Now," Leo growled at who I was assuming was a man.

"Give me your money and she doesn't get hurt," the man spoke, but instead a cloud of foul-smelling breath greeted my nose. Holy crap, this man needed to back off of me, and take shower.

His comment seemed to have made Leo even madder. Leo walked closer to us, his hand etching towards his pocket. "I'm not giving you anything. Let go of my girl," his voice was deep and terrifying. I wasn't sure why the man holding me couldn't just let go and walk away from the situation.

I don't think my mind was processing the situation I was in, or maybe my brain just blocked out the fact that I was being held by some random man. I could feel my heartbeat pick up however, once I realized that the man was holding a metal object against the side of my head. That was when I realized the situation I was in.

"Don't!" Leo shouted at the man when he noticed the weapon held against my temple. I could feel the tears flowing down my cheeks, but I needed to be smart. I had to think of a way to escape this psychopath's hold.

"Give me your money or she dies!" the man holding me screamed. I winced at the loud sound next to my ear.

I made eye contact with Leo, and he motioned with his eyes around us. That was when I noticed the guards that were surrounding the area, that the man seemed to not have noticed. I saw Leo reaching further into the pocket of his jacket and it dawned on me that Leo was reaching for his gun. He was armed at the restaurant. He was armed while shopping. He was armed while I was walking hand in hand with him. Was his lifestyle really that dangerous that he had to carry a gun with him at all times?

I was beyond thankful that he had it, don't get me wrong. I just don't understand how I was oblivious to think that a dangerous man like Leo wouldn't be armed at all times. I know he had to have it with him, but it was a freaking gun for God's sake.

I mentally cleared my thoughts, trying to focus on what was important at the moment which was trying to get myself out of this situation. I wasn't wearing any heels so I couldn't stab the man's foot with them, but I could kick his knee in. So that was what I decided to do.

I looked at Leo catching his eyes before looking down and then looking back up, hoping that he understood what I was trying to communicate to him. He seemed to have understood the plan and he gave me a slight nod. At least I hoped he understood it. Regardless, it was go time.

"How much do you want?" Leo asked the man, trying to buy me some time to get into position. I needed to get low enough to the point where either the guards or Leo could get a clean shot without me in the way. At the moment, the man had his back pressed against the wall with my back against his front. He was using me as a shield so if anyone shot, it would hit me as well.

I still noticed the guards around us, whispering orders through their earpieces. They probably already had a plan in place, but too bad mine was going to be the one to save me.

"Everything, just give me every-everything you have," the man screamed again. He was starting to get shaky, and I think the adrenaline was beginning to wear off of him.

I decided it was now or never, so I lifted my leg pressing it against his knee. I needed to make sure that I got the hit in the correct place, or else it probably wouldn't do anything to him and I would end up with a bullet through my head.

I pulled my knee back, letting out a breath before slamming it into his knee cap hearing a disgusting 'crack'. The man screamed in agony, and I took this as my chance to throw his arms off of me and run to where Leo was. I threw myself behind Leo, sobs leaving me. I freed myself. I really am a bad bi*ch.

The guards rushed over to the man, kicking his gun away while they all had their guns pointed at him.

"Easy, don't shoot," Leo's voice cut through, "I want him alive." He walked over to the man, leaving me where I was standing before taking the gun out of his pocket and hitting the man in the head with it causing him to fall unconscious.

"Bring him to the warehouse and have him ready for me to deal with him later. Feel free to bruise him up," Leo ordered venomously. He looked terrifying, and I wasn't one hundred percent sure what they were going to do to the man, but I did know that it was going to be awful. I didn't allow myself to think too much about it. If given the chance, this man would've killed me. And for what? Some money?

Leo turned towards me, pulling me into his chest. His arms were tight around my body, and I felt his breath on the top of my head. I wrapped my arms around Leo as well, my crying had stopped just by the comfort Leo offered me.

Leo led me to the car, still not letting go of my waist and allowed me to get into the car first before getting in himself. I immediately threw myself back into his arms.

"How are you feeling sweetheart?" he asked me in a gentle tone.

I sniffled, "I'm scared. I don't want to be alone right now."

"Shhh, you're never alone baby. I'm right here. Everything will be okay. We'll go to your house where you can shower, and put on some comfy pajamas. We'll get some food, and if you want I can call the girls to come over. Does that sound good?" He asked me, rubbing his hands up and down my arms.

I nodded my head, my hands becoming gradually shakier, but I kept them gripping Leo's shirt. And Leo was right, a nice, warm shower sounded amazing at the moment. "Yeah, that sounds nice. Thank you."

He kissed the top of my head, "Anything for you sweetheart."

Poor baby Aria :((but i hope you guys enjoyed, and sorry about the wait! Thank you for all the comments and votes, and please feel free to leave some on this chapter! Next chapter you're gonna see the real don inside of leo ;) happy reading! Also if anyone of you, or you know someone who makes covers for books please let me know!

Chapter 23

I think I blacked out for most of the car ride because one second we were driving the streets of New York, and the next we were at my house. I was trying to keep my cool in front of Leo, but honestly, I was freaking out on the inside.

The fear from the moment the gun was placed against my head remained at the pit of my stomach, and I think it was only getting worse. That man could have shot me. I could have been dead right now. And as much as I'd like to think that Leo wouldn't have let it come to that point, no one would've been able to stop that trigger from being pulled.

The fear was somewhat less there when I was in Leo's arms in a closed space. However, the moment I got out of the car and was exposed to the open darkness that surrounded my house, I couldn't help but look over my shoulder every couple of seconds to make sure no one would snatch me up in the night. Luckily, Leo seemed to have noticed and he walked behind me which did wonders to ease my overthinking mind.

My parents weren't home as they were invited over to one of their friend's houses for dinner and cocktails. Therefore, Leo and I were alone in the giant, dark house. The same house that had plenty of spaces for someone to hide.

Before we could walk any further I stopped. My overthinking made me way too sketched out by the house. "Leo, do you think we could check the house just to make sure everything is... okay?" I asked him, keeping my head down, too embarrassed that I sounded like a little kid who was asking their parent to check under the bed for monsters.

I felt a hand underneath my chin, lifting my head up to meet a gorgeous pair of blue ones. "Of course we can sweetheart. How about we do it together?"

I nodded my head at his question and that's what we did. We went through every room, bathroom, and closet in the house, Leo holding my hand the entire time we did it. My mind was able to chill knowing there wasn't anyone lurking around anywhere. Plus the guards at the entrances eased my mind definitely as well.

The last room we checked was mine, and when we got there Leo led me to the bathroom immediately. He turned on the shower while I awkwardly stood there.

He used his hand to check the temperature of the water, "Okay, the water is hot like you love it. I'll find you some pajamas and you can shower while I do that." He told me, placing a kiss on my forehead before moving to exit the bathroom. Before he could, I grabbed his wrist stopping him.

"When you come back, can you stay here with me?" I felt comfortable with the house, but there was no way I wanted to be alone anywhere at the moment.

He nodded, "Of course, I'll grab the clothes and then I'll come back in here. Is that okay?"

I let out a quiet 'yeah', and he walked out of the room, giving me a chance to get into the shower. The water was hot, just how I liked it and my heart warmed at the thought that Leo remembered such an insignificant thing.

As the coconut smell from my shampoo invaded my senses, I couldn't help but think about how quickly things change. Less than 24 hours ago we were enjoying Leo's birthday, which was such an amazing night, and then I was being held against my will by a man who was threatening my life for some money. Life works in mysterious ways.

I whipped my head towards the door when I heard a knock on it. The door wasn't closed in the first place, but it was Leo coming into the bathroom with my clothes. I was confused at how Leo was able to find the pajamas so quickly in the closet, but that was the least of my worries.

"Can I come in?" he asked me, keeping his gaze locked on the ground.

"Yeah," I called out to him.

I observed him as he walked across the marble tile, placing the clothes on the countertop before taking a seat on the toilet next to him. I noticed him pull out his phone before he started doing something on it.

I went back to showering, making sure that I scrubbed harder around my waist and neck. The places where that sorry excuse of a man placed his hands on me. My body was red by the time the shower was done.

I turned the shower off, going back to watching Leo. At hearing the shower turn off, he placed his phone back into his pocket, before grabbing the towel that was also on the counter next to him. He walked towards me, never letting his gaze wander up.

"Here's a towel. How about you walk me through your nighttime routine?" he suggested to me, but I knew it was a way to try and take my mind off of the earlier events. I nodded my head anyway, a slight smile forming on my face at the thought of Leo learning my vigorous night time regime.

He turned around while I dried off and got dressed into the cotton shorts and oversized sweatshirt he found in my closet. It definitely brought my mood up, especially when Leo kept asking me about the products and where I put them. He even offered to help spray some of the products in my hair for me.

"So this is how to stay so soft?" he asked me, pecking my cheek while rubbing my arm.

I let out a little laugh, "Basically. Maybe you should try some of these with me?"

"To have soft skin like yours? I'll try anything," he smirked at me, leaning against the counter.

I smiled as well before I turned serious again. "Leo, thank you for helping me feel better."

"Sweetheart, there's nothing in this world I want than for you to feel one hundred percent amazing. And however long that takes, I will be here to help you. You don't have to thank me," he pulled me into his arms, "Now I think your friends should be here soon with some food, so let's go out into the room and set up."

I hugged him tightly, pressing my face into his chest before pulling away and nodding my head. We walked back out into the room, and I took a seat on the bed meanwhile Leo grabbed some extra pillows and placed them on the floor by the couch.

The door to the room opened, and standing there were my three best friends in the entire world with some McDonald's.

"Hey Aria, we brought your favorite," Elena said, holding the bag towards me.

"Thank you," I said, walking up to them and pulling all three of them into a hug.

I was happy that Leo decided to call them over tonight. There's something about a good girls night in that helps the soul.

The girls began getting comfortable on the floor, setting out the food for us to eat. Meanwhile, I was saying goodbye to Leo.

"I'll only be gone for a couple of hours, but then I'll come by again," he reassured me.

"Okay, please don't take too long," I wrapped my arms around his waist pulling him into a tight hug. He wrapped his arms around me as well, and I inhaled his cologne.

We pulled away from the hug, "Enjoy your time with your friends, and before you know it, I'll be back." He kissed my lips before pulling away, "I love you."

"I love you too," I told him. Just like that, he was gone and I went back to eating and chatting with my friends.

Leo's POV

As soon as I closed the door behind me, my phone started ringing.

"Damon, is that bastard awake yet?" I growled, my anger quickly building.

"He's beginning to stir," I heard my closest friend reply on the other side.

"Good, I'm on my way," I hung up and got into the car.

My phone began ringing again, but this time it was my dad. I answered the call, "Yes father?"

"I heard what happened to Aria, I assume that you're going to the warehouse now?" He asked me. My dad knows me too well.

"You assumed correctly, he's gonna pay for what he put her through," I said venomously. My hands were aching to do some real damage to that piece of sh*t.

I heard my dad laugh on the other end, "Try not to stretch out his death too long."

I smirked, "No promises."

The ride to the warehouse was short, much to my pleasure. I threw open the car door, getting out quickly and walking into the warehouse.

"Boss," some of the guards greeted me at my arrival.

"Where is he?" I hissed, no longer having any patience.

One guard nodded but avoided eye contact with me; the way I liked it. "Follow me."

He led me to the open area of the warehouse. All my men were standing there, but they split and created a walkway for me when they noticed my presence. I noticed Damon up at the front of the crowd standing next to the sorry excuse of a man. I began removing my jacket, throwing it off to the side.

I noticed the man's eyes were still closed. Time to wake this trash up. I walked up to him, landing a hard punch to the side of the head. He cried out and opened his eyes.

"Wake up," I growled. Once he noticed me he tried to get out of the rope that was keeping him to the chair, but there was no use.

"From that look on your face, you seem to remember me which is good. I want you to remember this face, after all, it will be the last one you ever see," I smirked at him. Oh, he was in for a treat tonight.

"Ple-Please, I'm so sorry. Please let me go," he begged, but it made me even madder.

I let out a malicious laugh, "Funny you say that. Earlier you didn't plan on letting my girl go, did you? Even when she begged, you didn't listen." As the words left my lips, I felt this monstrous anger come over me. He put my Aria through hell tonight and he was going to pay in the worst way I knew how.

"I wasn't going to do anything to her, I just wanted some mo-money. Please," he cried to me, but it just pissed me off. I threw another punch to his face.

"Lies," I growled in his face. "Your gun was loaded. She would've been dead if you pulled that trigger. The last boy that left here went without a couple fingers and toes and that was for calling her a name. You almost took her life, what do you think your punishment will be?"

"Please, I'm sor-sorry. I'm so sorry, please, I'm begging you," he cried.

I grabbed a pair of sharp bush trimmers, before grabbing his hand. "I'm sure you are sorry, maybe I'll be sorry when you begin losing fingers. Then again, I'm not feeling remorseful tonight."

"Someone put me up to this!" he cried out before I could remove his ring finger.

"What are you talking about?" I growled.

"Someone pai-paid me. They gave me the gun and told me what to do. They offered me five hundred thousand if I scar-scared the girl. They told me they would get me out of any trouble I would get into. I wasn't going to kill her, I needed the money," he rushed out. What the hell was he saying?

"Who? What did the man look like?" I demanded, pressing my hand against his throat closing his windpipe.

The man choked, "He didn't tell me a name, he just said it was an offer from the Russians."

I let go of his throat, watching as he tried catching his breath.

That didn't make any sense. Why would the Russians want to hurt Aria? We were allies.

I looked back at the man who stared back at me with fear in his eyes, "I guess we'll just have to send them a message back then."

After hours of torture, I realized the man's story checked out. He didn't have any ties to the Russians other than what he told me.

I was wiping off my hands when my phone rang. I saw it was Aria and I quickly answered it.

"Hello, sweetheart is something wrong?" I asked her, worry etched in my voice.

I heard giggling on the other line, "Leooooooo, what are you doing? Are you coming back soon?" Her sweet voice asked me, immediately putting a smile on my face.

"Baby, did you guys drink something?" I had a smirk on my face.

"Maybeeee," she giggled again, "come back, I miss you. I wanna snuggle and kiss."

I wasn't worried about anyone seeing the large smile on my face due to the love of my life on the other side of the phone. I wasn't ever going to hide my affection towards her.

"I'll be there in an hour tops sweetheart," I assured her. "I love you."

"I love you too cupcake," she busted out laughing, "Oh my God I just called you cupcake." She then hung up the phone.

I walked back over to the man that was barely hanging onto his life. "Well my girl wants me home so I'll wrap this up," I pulled the gun out of the waistband of my jeans, and pointed it at him, shooting it.

The loud 'bang' rang through the room, "Clean this up. Damon follow me."

Damon walked next to me as we left, meanwhile I noticed some of my men begin cleaning up. We reached the car and got in, "Call my father so we can tell him what we found out. I gotta run home to shower and change."

He nodded before calling, and I explained everything that happened tonight.

"Good work son, we'll have a meeting about this tomorrow. I'm heading to bed, I'll see you tomorrow," my dad hung up the phone.

We reached my house and I took the quickest shower of my life before driving back to Arias. Damon had left to go home, so it was me alone in the car.

Once I got to Aria's, I walked upstairs noticing that her friends were passed out in the theater room. I finally got to her room and noticed her laying on the bed, absentmindedly tracing her fingers on the soft covers. I knocked on the door to get her attention.

"Hey baby, you didn't have to wait up for me. It's late," I got into bed, sliding under the covers.

"I know, but my parents decided to stay in the city for the night and I couldn't fall asleep without you next to me," she snuggled into me. I noticed her long eyelashes, how they curl naturally and framed her large eyes so well. God, she was the most beautiful girl I ever had the pleasure of looking at.

She lifted her head so I could see her pretty face. Her eyes kept glancing down at my lips, something that she did when she wanted to be kissed. Before she could even ask, I leaned down meeting her lips with my own. The kiss was passionate, and I knew deep in my bones that I would do anything for her.

There was no place I'd rather be than with my girl.

I hope you guys enjoyed the little mix up of point of views in this chapter! let me know if you would wanna see more chapters in Leo's point of view. also I just made a plan for this story and there's only a couple more chapters left and I hope to have the entire book finished by Aug 1st when I go on vacation! get ready for rapid updates!! again I want to say thank you for the insane amount of support and I love all of you!!

Chapter 24

The days leading up to the last day of school came rather quickly. Finals were a blur and before I knew it, it was the official last day of my Junior year.

On the last day, we're allowed to wear whatever we want and ditch the ugly uniforms until the next school year. So I decided to wear a tight, mini denim skirt along with a woven, white, cropped tank top and I layered on gold necklaces. Since the weather was finally getting hot, I was able to start bringing out all of my summer clothing.

Most days on the way to school I would be quite miserable. However, since it was the last day, I couldn't help the smile that was on my face. Plus, Leo was picking me up this morning so that also might've had something to do with my good mood.

When he texted me saying that he was here, I practically skipped down the stairs. I was in such a good mood that I kissed my mom on the cheek when I passed her on my way out. I just knew that today was going to be a great day.

I walked out of the house to see Leo leaning against the car with a panini and strawberry drink in his hands. My favorites. I made my way towards him with a huge smile on my face.

"Did you get me breakfast?" I asked him, standing on my toes to kiss him.

"I sure did, considering that you slept through your alarm and only woke up when I called you like five times. I figured you wouldn't have time to eat anything," he joked.

I laughed, "What can I say? The handsome man in my dreams made it hard to wake up."

"I sure hope that man had dark black hair, blue eyes, and was named Leonardo," he tried joking, but I picked up on the tone of jealousy within his voice.

I rolled my eyes, "Of course it was you silly." I pecked him on the cheek. Actually, it was Harry Styles, but what Leo didn't know wouldn't hurt him.

"Alright, well we should get going. We're already going to be late," he said looking down at his watch before he opened the car door for me.

"Who cares, it's the last day of school baby," I said with a smile. The school was lucky enough that I even decided to go today.

The whole ride there I was singing rather loudly to songs from my phone that I forced Leo to play on the AUX. Leo, although he kept praising that I was a good singer, looked miserable the whole way there.

As soon as we arrived, I took Leo's hand and led him over to my locker where I knew the girls were waiting for me. Only there were four more people standing there than normal. Damon, Justin, Vince, and even Margot were standing with the girls at the locker.

"What's up bi*ches," I said loud enough for them to hear me.

"You seem pretty happy Aria," Claire said, surprised at my outburst.

Leo pulled me in closer to him, "Tell me about it, she was pretty much bouncing around the whole car ride."

"It's the last day of school, it's like my third favorite day in the year," I defended myself.

"What's your first two?" Vince asked.

"My birthday, and New Year's Eve," I responded.

Vince nodded, "Hmm, noted."

"Anyways," Elena moved along the conversation, "today they're having a little picnic thing in the courtyard, so we can chill there for a little and then we can go to a lake or someone's house?"

Everyone nodded, agreeing to the plans. We made our way out to the courtyard where students were doing the activities and eating food. It looked like a carnival type of scene.

"Oh my God, they decorated it so nice out here," Victoria gushed, and I agreed with her. It looked amazing outside.

"What do you wanna go do first sweetheart?" Leo asked me.

I looked around, trying to see what picked up my interest first before my eyes landed on the Hula Hoop competition. "Oh, we have to go do that," I pointed to the little table.

"Well, let's do it then," Leo said, and we walked over to the table.

"Hey ya'll, do you think you have what it takes to win Mr. Kitty?" The woman working the table said in an overly excited tone while motioning over to the giant, stuffed cat.

I immediately nodded my head; I knew I had what it takes to win. We decided that it would be Vince, Justin, Elena, Damon, Victoria, and I taking part in the competition.

"Are you gonna be my cute, little cheerleader?" I asked Leo before the competition started.

"Of course baby, I'll be cheering you on from the sidelines," he smirked pressing a kiss to my forehead. "Make daddy proud," he whispered to me in a husky tone.

I fake gagged at the word he used, pushing him away. He walked back to where the rest were standing, laughing on the way there. I felt my cheeks get hot, but I needed to focus on the prize. I wanted Mr. Kitty.

"Alright, so the last person still hula-hooping wins, so, good luck," the woman said before blowing a blow horn signaling the start of the competition.

I was able to pick up a solid rhythm which would allow me to stay in the competition for longer. Right away Justin got out of the competition, and shortly after Elena followed. Victoria distracted Vince, which led to him getting out. It was just Victoria, Damon, and I left in the game. That was until Vince bumped into Victoria to get her out. Then it was just Damon and me left. I narrowed my eyes at him. I guess hula hooping was a secret talent of his.

I was starting to get a little bit tired, but I couldn't give up. I was already too invested in this competition. Damon's hula hoop began slipping down him, and he tried lifting it back up but it was too late. Damon was out, and I was the winner.

"Whoo-hoo!" I screamed, holding the hula hoop above my head.

The woman handed Mr. Kitty over to me, and I gladly took it running over to Leo. "I won!" I screamed and he lifted me off the ground.

"That's my girl!" he beamed at me. "You did so well out there, I'm so proud."

I laughed before he put me down and the rest of the group congratulated me as well. Was this a little bit dramatic because it was literally just a small hula hooping competition? Yes. Did I mind the attention or the bragging rights I gained as a result? Nope.

We continued going through and playing a bunch of the games. By the end of it, my arms were full of stuffed animals, and even Leo was holding some as well.

"For the next game can Leonardo and Aria please sit out?" Claire sighed.

I looked at her confused, "Why?"

"Because you and Leonardo are literally good at everything, and I want a stuffed animal too," Elena said with a fake frown.

I laughed and Leo pulled me closer to him, "If my girl wants one of those stuffed teddy bears, than who am I to deny her it?" Leo mocked, and I kissed him on the cheek.

"We'll sit out, but only because we can't hold any more prizes," I rubbed it in their faces.

We eventually got bored with the carnival and Justin invited everyone back to his house to chill out. We ended up ordering some pizza, and everyone sat around eating and talking. It was a fun way to welcome summer, and I was truly happy I got to do it with my friends, new and old.

When it got later into the night, we decided to have a bonfire in his backyard. I had a blanket wrapped around my shoulders, sitting down on one of the benches that surrounded the fire pit, next to Leo. He immediately wrapped his arms around me, allowing me to snuggle into him.

"I had a lot of fun today," I told him, looking around and noticing how everyone was interacting with each other.

"I did too, but I always have a good time when I'm with you," he told me. I laughed at the cheesiness of his comment, but it still managed to make a blush appear on my cheeks.

"I actually wanted to ask you something Aria," he told me before pulling an envelope out of his pocket. "I already asked your parents and they're okay with it."

My heart began racing, "Oh my God, Leo are you proposing me?" I asked him starting to panic.

"What? Aria no I'm not proposing. Do you really think I would do it with an envelope in front of a fire?" he sounded slightly offended.

"I don't know, you said that my parents agreed and my mind jumped to that right away," I shrugged.

He shook his head, "When I propose to you, it will be extravagant, but that's for another day. Open the envelope."

I took the envelope from his hands noticing a travel itinerary in it. "What is this?" I asked him before I noticed my name and Greece on it, "Oh my God, are we going to Greece?"

"We are, I wanted to surprise you with a trip, and we'd be back before your birthday. So, what do you say?" He looked kind of nervous but I knew my answer.

"Hell yeah, I'll go. I've never been to Greece before!" I jumped into his arms with a huge smile on my face that he shared as well.

"We're going to Greece!" I told the group, and they all shared the same happiness as we did.

The rest of the night was pretty chill, and I just kept thinking about the beach and Leo shirtless on the beach. This was going to be an amazing summer.

Hope you enjoyed! Next chapter is coming tomorrow :) Thank you for all the support! i love you all !!

Chapter 25

Spicy content towards the end, things are heating up! You've been warned.

"Mom, the suitcase won't close!" I yelled, huffing at my failed attempt to fit all of my things into two suitcases.

"You're packing all of that? I thought you were only going for a week," my mom's voice sounded confused.

I wiped a bead of sweat off of my forehead, "We are."

"Then why do you have two suitcases overflowing?" she asked me.

"Mom, I need to have a good variety of clothing while I'm there. I need something for every occasion. Now help me close this," I ordered her, trying my best to pack down the clothes.

"Leo's supposed to be here soon, why did you wait so long to pack?" she asked me, now trying to pack down the clothes with me.

My mind flashed to all the times that Leo came over to "help me pack", but it usually ended with makeout sessions on my bed.

"Yeah, I have no idea," I told her, clearing my mind of those moments.

She finally was able to get the zipper to close on the second suitcase, "I sure hope that boy knows what he's getting into with an over-packer like you."

"Same here, but he loves me so he'll have to get used to it," I shrugged my shoulders.

"On the topic of love, why don't we have a conversation," she said, walking over to the bed and taking a seat.

"A conversation about what?" I asked, confused by what she meant.

"Well, you're going somewhere romantic with your boyfriend, and sometimes the emotions go crazy and you're so in love and blah, blah, blah, you just have to be careful," she spoke freely.

Meanwhile, I had a traumatized look on my face, "Mom, we're not gonna do anything like... that." My face was red, and I was embarrassed that we were having a conversation like this.

"You know your father took me on a trip like the one you're going on when we-"

"Mom!" I screeched, I think my ears began bleeding.

"Alright, I'll stay quiet, but all I'm saying is if you decide to do anything, please be careful," she said beginning to stand up.

"Noted. Now if you'll excuse me, I think I'm going to be sick to my stomach." I said, pretending to gag.

She just laughed before walking out of the room. My face was still red, I can't believe that she thought Leo and I would be doing anything of that... nature.

I mean, I'm sure that we eventually will but would this trip be one of those times? My phone started ringing which, thankfully, took my thoughts away from the embarrassment.

"Hello?" I answered the phone, not bothering to see who it was.

"Hey baby," I heard his deep voice on the other side of the phone, "Are you all packed up?"

I looked around my room which was a total mess, noticing that all my face products and shoes were still unpacked. "Yeah, pretty much."

"Okay, I'll be there in about an hour to pick you up and then we'll head to the airport," he said.

I began panicking. I only had an hour to get my life together, "Alright, I'll see you soon." I ended the call and ran around trying to fit everything else into another empty suitcase.

That hour definitely flew by way too quickly, because the next thing I knew, Leo was knocking on the door and I was struggling to close the third suitcase.

"Aria, what are you doing?" he asked me, clearly confused.

"Oh great, you're here. Here help me close this one and we can go," I ordered him to help me close the suitcase.

"Do you always pack this much for vacations?" he asked, walking over to where the suitcase was, attempting to close it himself.

I took a seat on the bed, exhausted by the tedious task of packing, "If you think this is bad, you should've seen how much I packed for our month trip to France."

"So buy another jet for your luggage when we go on longer trips in the future. Noted," he joked, causing me to laugh.

"Do you have everything you need?" he asked me and I nodded. "I'll send someone to come up and grab all of your luggage before we leave."

I handed him my backpack that held all my chargers and headphones before we walked downstairs. "Mom, I think we're gonna head out," I called out to her.

Her and my dad both came into the foyer. "Hope you kids have a fun time. Enjoy the beach, Aria maybe try to get a little bit of tan," my mom gushed pulling the both of us into hugs. I laughed at her comment because I knew I wouldn't get tan.

My dad was next to pull us into a hug, "Have fun kids. Leo make sure you take care of my daughter."

"With my life sir," Leo responded and I noticed a smirk of satisfaction on my dad's face at his response. Men.

"I love you guys, I'll see you soon," I told the two of them, to which they replied with 'love you too's'.

Soon enough we were on one of the Moretti's planes flying to Mykonos, Greece.

I don't remember when I fell asleep on the plane, but I do remember waking up and realizing that I was leaning against Leo and my neck was now sore.

"How long have I been asleep," I asked him, sitting up and wiping some drool off of my face.

"For a couple of hours. We're almost in Madrid so we can fuel back up," he said, wrapping his arm around my shoulders.

I nodded, noticing he had his laptop out, "What are you doing?"

"I'm looking over some of the documents that my dad sent over to me regarding the Russians and the possible link on why they'd want to hurt either of us, but I can't find anything," his voice sounded frustrated.

Leo ended up telling me what the Russians did when that man held a gun to my head, and as normal I was quite freaked out by it. None of us knew why the Russians would plan something like that or why they tried to kill Leo, but there definitely was some sort of war brewing.

"You and your dad will figure this out Leo, you'll get to the bottom of it," I encouraged him. I wasn't sure how these things were typically handled, but I still offered my support where it was needed.

"I know baby," he closed his laptop, "I don't want to stress out. This is our time, and no one will come in the middle of that." He pecked me on the lips, but I reached my hands out to cup his face to deepen the kiss before I pulled back.

"Exactly, all your attention is mine this week," I joked with him.

He let out a little chuckle, "yes ma'am. What are you most excited about this trip?"

I thought about it for a second, "spending quality time with you, seeing Mykonos for the first time, and having unlimited access to you shirtless."

This made him let out a loud laugh, "Sweetheart, you can see me shirtless whenever you want, you just have to ask."

I shrugged, "I know but this time I have an excuse. What are you most excited about?"

"Spending time with my girl, that's all I'm ever excited about," he smiled cheesily at me, causing me to laugh.

"You're so cheesy."

He shrugged innocently, "It's not my fault I'm so in love with you."

We spent most of the flight and even the layover in Madrid just talking and watching movies. Now we were about fifteen minutes from landing in Mykonos.

"Oh my gosh, it's already so pretty outside," I gushed, noticing the bright blue water and how excited I was to go for a swim in it.

"You'll be happy to know that our little bungalow is located right next to the private beach I rented out for us. So we won't have to worry about prying eyes," I knew that he was the only one that worried about prying eyes, but I guess I wouldn't want anyone eyeballing my eye candy either.

Soon enough we landed and were on our way to the bungalow. Just driving around Mykonos I was in complete awe. It was beautiful. The buildings had so much character and the white was such a strong contrast against the blue water.

We pulled up to what I assumed would be our bungalow, but I was expecting a little room with a bed. If this was Leo's idea of a bungalow then I was thoroughly surprised. The "bungalow" we would be staying at was huge. It overlooked the beach and was decorated with typical beachy furniture. The house was two stories and my favorite part was one of the balconies in the master bedroom that overlooked the city. I knew this view would be beautiful at night. There was also another balcony that overlooked the water that Leo seemed to grow a liking too.

"So, do you like it?" he asked me with a huge smile.

"Like it? Leo, I love it, I'm scared I'm never going to want to go home ever again," I jumped on the bed, falling onto my back.

Our suitcases had already been brought up to the room and were neatly placed off to the side next to the closet.

"What do you want to do first?" he asked me.

"Do you think we could go down to the beach and order some food?" I suggested.

"Of course," he got up and moved to one of his suitcases, grabbing what looked like swim trunks, "I'll change in the bathroom real quick."

He practically ran into the bathroom and I noticed how excited he seemed. I got off the bed and moved over to the smaller suitcase where I put all of my swimsuits. I had a lot of options to choose from, but I ultimately decided on one. It was a snakeskin bikini. The top was a wide strapped, swooped style while the bottoms were high waisted, but they definitely were cheeky. I mean they showed a lot of booty, but it looked good and I was on vacay, so why not flaunt?

I heard the door to the bathroom open as I was sliding the top of my bikini over my head. I quickly turned away from the bathroom door, "Hold on I'm still changing!"

The top to the bikini was tight so I had a hard time trying to get it over my breasts. "Leo, can you pull down the back for me?"

"Um, yeah sure," he replied. I heard footsteps walking towards where I was struggling before I felt his hands pull down the back of the swimsuit. It was officially covering my chest.

"Thank you," I said, turning back around. His cheeks were slightly red, and he just nodded.

"You ready to go?" he asked me. I nodded and we walked out of the hut and onto the sand. The weather was beautiful and warm; I could already feel the sun penetrating into my skin. There was a seating area set up in a large white tent with a giant, circle, seating couch thing in the middle. This was where I would be staying to ensure that I didn't burn while we were on the beach.

"Do you know what you want to eat? I'll call in the order," Leo told me, hopping on the phone that was next to the little seating area.

"Yep, strawberry lemonade and chicken tenders with fries." It was a basic order but man was I craving it.

He called in our order and once that was done I pulled him up to go into the water with me. The water was warm, and it felt refreshing against my warm skin. Leo dived under the water, meanwhile, I remained above the surface because I can't swim.

We stayed in the water, splashing around, kissing, before our food was ready and we went back to eat. Then we went back into the water before we were exhausted. Along with the jetlag and the activities of today, I was ready for a nap.

However, I wasn't ready to go in yet. I couldn't stop staring at Leo's abs the whole time we were on the beach, and honestly, I wasn't even ashamed about it. Not when I noticed Leo countless times staring at my chest and behind.

We were back in the little tent area, sitting side by side on the couch thing, trying to dry off.

"Thank you for bringing me on this trip Leo," I said breaking the silence.

"Anything for you sweetheart. Plus I can't complain, seeing you in these bikinis all week is a treat all on its own," he smirked, lightly running his hand up my exposed hip. I couldn't help the butterflies that erupted in my stomach at the feeling.

"I have much saucier ones where that came from," I told him, deciding to tease him.

Next thing I know, I was on my back and he was hovering over me, using his arms to support himself. "You are quite the tease, aren't you Aria," he whispered huskily.

I went to respond before my lips were stolen into a kiss. A quite passionate one at that. It was soon a full flown makeout session, and I definitely wasn't complaining. I wrapped my legs around his waist, bringing his lower region closer to mine. My hands were roaming his hair, while his hands were gripping my behind.

I felt his hand start tracing my stomach, moving further south. I knew where this was going, we just hadn't ever done anything like this before. At the moment, however, I wanted nothing more than for him to put his hand on the place that I needed him the most.

He pulled away from the kiss for a second stopping his hand from going any lower, "We should probably stop."

"I don't want to stop," I murmured, trying to catch my breath.

"Are you sure?" he asked me, still hesitant.

I nodded, "Yes, I want you, Leo."

His eyes turned darker and his lips went back to attacking my own. His hand reached below the waistband of my swimsuit, and I let out a moan at the feeling. I had touched myself down there before, but his hands doing it just felt amazing.

I pulled away from the kiss, throwing my head back and arching my back. Leo's lips were attacking my neck and loud moans were leaving mine. I wasn't going to last much longer.

I felt Leo's fingers speed up before I let out one last moan, reaching my high. Leo moved his fingers out from my waistband, moving to lay back down next to me, pulling me into his side.

"Holy crap, that was amazing," I said still out of breath.

"There's a lot more where that came from baby," he said, pressing a kiss to my forehead.

This was most definitely going to be a trip to remember.

This chapter definitely made me excited for my vacation, but I hope you all enjoyed! Only two more chapters left, but the next chapter will definitely be a long one!! Also, we hit 102K reads which is so insane. Thank you to everyone that's been reading, and supporting Young God!! It means so much to me! Love you all, see you tomorrow!

Chapter 26

The rest of the night was spent walking around the city, and getting some dinner. Luckily things between Leo and I weren't awkward even after the ... things we did. I felt that in some way Leo and I had become even closer, I mean he did have his hands down my pants. I just felt even more comfortable with him than before. I don't think I was ready to actually do the real thing yet, but I was okay with where things were at the moment.

The rest of the trip flew by way too quickly for my liking. I mean don't get me wrong, it was spent in pure bliss for the majority of it, I was just sad that it was over so soon. My birthday was a week away so that was something I needed to plan, but I loved my birthday so it wasn't a chore at all. I still hadn't decided on a theme for my birthday, but I needed to go all out since it was my eighteenth.

As soon as Leo and I got back to New York, he was busy doing work for his father since it was summer and he didn't have school to get in the way. Meanwhile, I met up with the girls to help plan my birthday and overall catch up on everything.

We were at our usual brunch place, this time, however, Margot joined us. Margot wasn't as outgoing as the rest of us so it was harder for us to try and crack her introverted shell, but we still made it our job to welcome her with open arms.

I had my notebook out for planning, but I was stumped on a theme for the party that was now only five days away. "Guys, I have no idea what I want to do for my birthday," I groaned, throwing my hands up.

"Why not just do like a pool party or something since it's July and hot as hell?" Claire asked me.

I immediately shook my head, "No that's too casual, I'm turning eighteen not throwing a party at a frat house."

"Well you like Gatsby and glam so why not do something around that?" Victoria chimed in this time.

I groaned, "I can't do that either because that was Leo's party theme. C'mon ladies, think bigger."

"You could do like a costume party," Margot suggested.

That piqued my interest. Everyone could dress however they wanted to, plus it was warm enough to wear any kind of costume without worrying about the weather.

"Is that weird to do it when it's not fall yet?" Claire asked.

Elena shook her head, "I don't think so. It's unique, plus who doesn't love to dress a little provocative from time to time?"

"I like that idea, I think I finally decided on the theme. Thank you, Margot!" I beamed at her, happy that this stress was finally lifted off of my shoulders. She smiled at me, and Elena gave her a kiss on the cheek. They were honestly so cute together.

"Now that you have that figured out Aria, tell us about the trip!" Elena said excitedly.

"It was good, we went to the beach, I still didn't tan-" I began.

"Yeah, we can tell," Claire cut in, forcing me to glare at her.

"Anyways, it was really nice. The little house we stayed at was beautiful, and it had the most amazing view from the balcony of the city and another of the water," I gushed to them.

"Did you and Leo do anything?" Victoria asked me, raising her brows.

I blushed, "Um, no we didn't."

"You're not very convincing Aria," Elena smirked, which caused my face to redden even more.

"Okay fine, we might've done... some things," I said quietly but I knew that their nosy asses heard me.

"Oh my God!" Claire squealed, causing us to shush her because a group of older women sent dirty looks our way, but she ignored us and their glares. "What did you guys do?"

"I mean he like, he did you know, that thing, with his fingers, you know where," by this point, my face was burning and I felt incredibly awkward. Why did my friends have to be so nosy?

"You're growing up so quick Aria," Victoria wiped a pretend tear away.

Claire leaned in closer, "Did you do anything to him?"

I shook my head, thinking about it. I didn't return anything to Leo the whole trip. "No I didn't, was I supposed to? He didn't ask for anything, and when I tried to pull a move he just said that it was about me. Do you think he doesn't want anything like that from me?" Of course, my mind was overthinking, the smallest thing and boom I was stressed out of my mind.

"Maybe he just wanted to focus on you Aria, I mean this trip was sort of your birthday gift so maybe that was his present?" Elena tried convincing me, but she sounded unsure of herself.

"Or maybe he just didn't want you to do anything to him, I mean that's okay too," Margot tried soothing my worries. However, their attempts just stressed me out more.

I looked to Claire, the one person I knew that had good enough experience in this field. "Claire, has that ever happened to you before?"

"I mean some of the guys I've been with wanted something in return if they did anything like that with me, but they were all do*ches too. Some guys just prefer giving over receiving, it happens," she shrugged. It did make me feel better, but I just decided not to let it get to me too much. I know that if Leo wasn't okay with something or if there was a problem he would talk to me about it.

"You're right, I'm just not going to worry about it. I have a birthday party to plan." I said sighing.

"So Vince and I slept together," Victoria burst out of nowhere.

"What?" we all shouted in unison. Just like that, the rest of the brunch was spent listening to Victoria's first time.

It was two days before my party and Leo and I were shopping for matching costumes. The only problem was that Leo was stubborn and picky.

"Leo, look how cute these are. We can be prisoners," I pointed at the orange pants.

"Absolutely not, we need to stand out," he stated shaking his head.

"I'm gonna stand out when I actually go to prison you annoying little-" I murmured to myself.

"Did you say something?" He asked me.

I shook my head, "Nope, you're hearing things." I loved Leo, but boy did I want to fight this man sometimes.

"What if I was a mobster and you were my wife," he suggested.

"Leo we can't dress up as things we're already going to be one day," I pointed out.

That was when my eyes caught a white, sparkly dress that was mini and had a large cut at the cleavage. There were large white, feather wings that came with the costume as well. I needed this in my life.

"Oh my God, Leo what if I was an angel and you dressed up like the devil?" I suggested showing him the costume that I was in love with.

"That costume is really nice," he said looking at the costume I was looking at, "I like that idea."

I squealed, happy that we decided on something. We found Leo's costume which was a silk, red suit with the devil horns. The idea was basic, but we were gonna look damn good at the party.

It was officially the day of the party, and surprisingly I wasn't as stressed as I thought I would be. Everything seemed to be going the way I wanted it to for the first time probably ever. The food was being made without complications, the decorations were up and ready, the only thing I was waiting for was to get my hair and makeup done by none other than Mack and Isabell.

I walked through the downstairs noticing how transformed the living and dining room were. There was grey fabric draped throughout, much like it was for Leo's party. They had spooky decorations throughout as well as a fog machine. It was basically a Halloween in July type of feel.

I was back in my room when I heard a knock at the door. I opened it and noticed Mack and Isabell there.

"Aria!" Mack squealed pulling me into a hug. I hugged her back, slightly amazed at how strong this woman was. When she let go of me, I pulled Isabell into a hug as well.

"I'm so happy you ladies were able to help me out tonight," I told them leading them into the room.

"We're happy you called Aria, happy birthday by the way!" Mack said, her short red hair swaying as she walked over to the window examining the lighting.

"Happy birthday Aria," Isabell said, much calmer than Mack.

"Thank you," I told them, before being gestured into the chair Mack had already set up.

"What are you wearing tonight?" she asked me, running her hands through my hair.

"I'm dressing as an angel," I told her, eyeing my costume that was off to the side. As soon as the words left my mouth, they went to work. My eyes were a white glitter and the lashes were dramatic. They did loose waves on my hair, overall giving me an angelic look.

Leo got here while Mack was still doing my hair, so Isabell added some fake blood on his neck to give him more of a devilish look. Soon enough we were ready to go. My costume fit my body like a glove, and the glitter that I added to my skin helped me look even more innocent.

Leo and I were total opposites, even beyond our costumes. Our costumes represented us so well, however, what it failed to show was the angel in Leo and the devil in me. We both brought out the best in each other while bringing out the crazy in each other as well. Whatever my life has in store for me, I knew I could handle it as long as I had him by my side.

He was holding my hand as we stood behind the door to the party.

"You ready?" he asked me.

"Always."

And so we entered the party.

This chapter is shorter, but honestly, I felt like a longer one would be too redundant of things that have already happened in the book, so sorry for lying about the long chapter. I hope you guys enjoyed, there's only one more chapter left!!!! Let me know how you think the book is gonna end because I'm curious to see if anyone picked up on the clues I've been leaving throughout! Anyways, thank you again for the support and see you tomorrow for the finale!

Chapter 27

Listen to sign of the times by harry styles towards the end of the chapter, it helped me write the ending

---

I was happy to see that no one else dressed up as a devil and angel, even though they are definitely classic costumes. I was also happy to see that everyone who attended the party went all out as well.

Everyone seemed to be having a good time from what I could tell just looking around the room. I noticed our little group standing by one of the tables so I pulled Leo along with me over to them. Claire and Justin were dressed up as a cheerleader and a jock. Victoria and Vince decided to be a Nun and Priest. Meanwhile, Elena and Margot dressed up in the signature plaid outfits from the movie Clueless. Damon and his date from Leo's party, Crystal, were dressed as lifeguards. I was thoroughly impressed with everyone's outfits.

"Aria, holy crap those wings are epic," Elena gushed when we walked up to the group. She stuck her hand out to touch the feathers and I couldn't blame her, they were incredibly soft.

"Thank you, you all look amazing," I gushed at them.

"Happy birthday by the way," Victoria said, before everyone else followed by saying 'Happy Birthday' as well.

"It's crazy, I'm officially an adult," I said, proud of the accomplishment of managing to stay alive for eighteen years. I didn't feel much different, but just knowing that I was eighteen made me feel grown.

"Have you seen the gifts table, it's like seriously overflowing," Justin said, pointing over to the table where it was in fact overflowing.

My eyes widened, "Holy crap, why is there so much?"

"Because people like you Aria," Claire said shrugging.

"I suppose."

"Anyways, I feel like there's a lot of people here that I don't recognize," Vince said which I frowned at.

"I only invited people from school, and no one was able to get in without their name on the list," I said, looking to Leo to see if he knew anything.

"It's probably just because we only hang out with each other. I mean in the halls I used to see new faces every day," Claire said, easing my mind because she was right. It was a big school, but I knew everyone that I invited including their plus ones. There was no way anyone could've gotten through security without their names on the list.

"Everything's fine sweetheart, there weren't any problems with security. I made sure to check beforehand," Leo said, comforting my stressed mind.

After the events that took place when Leo and I were shopping, I was still wary of everyone around me. The problem with the Russians was still unsolved, so I would rather be safe than sorry regarding who was allowed to enter my house.

"Let's just enjoy the night and have a good time. I only get to turn eighteen once," I joked with them.

"Amen to that sis," Elena said raising her drink.

After that, I went and talked to my parents as well as Leo's. They were mingling with the older crowd, but they still decided to dress up. My mom was a nurse, while my father was a doctor. Steven dressed up as a mobster, while Sofia dressed like a mob wife. I guess like father like son.

"Happy birthday sweetheart," Sofia said pulling me into a hug. I hugged her back, thanking her before I was pulled into a hug by Steven.

"Happy eighteenth birthday Aria, it's a big day for you!" he smiled at me.

"Thank you, Steven," I smiled back. It was hard to think that Steven was this big, bad mafia man when honestly he was one of the nicest people I have ever met.

"Oh what fitting costumes," Sofia said laughing. I laughed too because it was true. Leo was wearing all red, meanwhile, I was wearing all white. We contrasted very strongly against each other.

"You're right mom, she is my angel after all," Leo said smirking at me. I rolled my eyes at his cheesiness, feeling the warmth from the blush that covered my cheeks.

"Ugh so cute. To be young and in love, it truly is amazing," my mom gushed.

"It's even better to be old and in love," my dad said kissing my mom on the forehead. I admired how close my parents were. I hope that when Leo and I are their age, we resemble my parents or even his; still in love despite all obstacles.

"I'm not old," my mom said, slapping my dad on the chest.

Steven laughed, "Why don't you two enjoy your youth and leave us oldies."

We laughed and said bye before walking back over to where our friends were. They were all laughing when we walked over to them.

"Oh my God, Aria remember that one sleepover when Claire fell asleep early and we drew on her face with eyeliner," Elena filled me in, laughing as she did.

I laughed, remembering the memory, "Oh, that was good. She left the next morning without even looking in the mirror, and she was having breakfast with her parents that day."

"Don't act so innocent Aria, remember that one time you got so drunk you were running down the street naked," Claire said with raised eyebrows.

"We were chasing after her for like ten minutes," Victoria said laughing.

I laughed remembering the videos they showed me, "Actually I don't remember, I woke up with the biggest headache the next day."

"So you've always been frisky with a couple of drinks in you," Leo whispered in my ear causing me to blush. He knows just how much I love his lips when I've had one too many drinks.

"You girls are wild," Justin said shaking his head.

"We're best friends, if you don't have wild memories, then are you even best friends?" Elena said, and I agreed. We had done some pretty crazy stuff together.

"There's actually this one time when Leo was so drunk he bought an island and wouldn't tell us why. His dad was so pissed," Damon said. It was so hard for me to imagine Leo being that drunk because I don't think I have ever seen him even tipsy before.

"Actually, there is a reason I bought that island," Leo said pulling a piece of paper out of his suit jacket, "it was before we started dating, but I knew that one day you would be mine. So I bought it."

"Leo," I said slowly not believing what he was saying, "what are your plans with that Island?"

"Actually, it's not my plans, it's yours. The island is yours Aria, you own it," he handed me the paperwork and there was, in fact, my named under the ownership of a freaking island.

"Leo. You bought me an island?" I asked him in shock.

"Yes I bought you an island," he confirmed kissing me on the cheek.

"A whole ass island?"

"Yes, Aria a whole island, for you."

"Like a piece of land, floating in the ocean. That's what you bought me."

"Well when you say it like that it doesn't sound as nice," he frowned, "do you not like it?"

"No. I mean yes I like it. Leo, you bought me an island. Thank you?" I said unsure of how to accept this gift.

"You're welcome, I know it's a big thing sweetheart, but you'll be able to do whatever you want with it. We can build a house there or something," Leo said, kissing my forehead.

"I don't know how I'll ever top the gift of a freaking island," I admitted.

"Sweetheart, you don't even have to give me gifts. You are more than enough."

I looked over at my friends who were in shock, "I own a freaking island."

Claire looked at Leo with wide eyes, "How rich are you?"

Victoria smacked her on the shoulder but I agreed with Claire. He literally got me an island, this man truly was something else.

My mom came over to our table, "Aria, I think it's time to start the cake."

I nodded, and we all got up, walking over to where there was a large table set up in the middle of the room with a huge cake on it. I walked behind the table with my parents and Leo next to me. My friends were in front of me while Leo's parents were off to the side.

They began singing happy birthday, but I zoned it out. I focused on the overwhelming feeling of seeing my loved ones here for me. The smile on my face was huge. I had never felt happier in my life. I leaned down, puckering my lips, getting ready to blow out the candles. I wished that this happiness wouldn't end, that this moment of joy wouldn't ever leave. But there's a reason why wishes are just wishes and not reality. The happiness left as soon as shots were heard throughout the room.

No one knew what was happening, but as soon as I heard the first scream I knew something wasn't right.

"Everyone get down!" someone screamed. I don't know who it was. I was frozen.

I felt my body get pulled down by Leo, who was mouthing something but I couldn't hear anything. What was going on? Why were people hiding?

I was taken out of my shock by Leo shaking my shoulders, "Aria are you okay?" His voice was frantic.

"I'm fine, what's going on?" I asked him, still confused by the situation.

"The Russians, they're here. I don't know how they got through," he was mad. His voice sounded angry. "Aria, you have to get out of here okay. They can't hurt you, I won't let them."

I started to panic, "Leo, I can't leave you. What if something happens to you?"

He looked hesitant, "I'll be fine, please Aria. Remember that favor you owe me? From all that time ago? I'm using it. You need to get out of here. Whatever happens to me, you need to leave and get out of here. I need to know you're safe. Most people made it out, but I need you to run when you get the chance."

I nodded, but I knew there was no way I could leave Leo alone down here.

He looked around the table, "Run next to me, I'll take you to the exit and then you have to leave. Aria, whatever happens, I love you. Please remember that always."

"I love you too Leo, please you can't leave me, you have to come back safe," I begged him. He only ignored my request placing a kiss on my lips. It was short, it was rushed.

"On the count of three we run," he ordered and I nodded. He took the gun out of his suit pocket, "One, two, three."

We jumped up and began running before we ran into a man who blocked our way. Leo pulled me behind me, using himself as a human shield.

"Leonardo, Aria where are you off to so soon?" the sick man smirked, pointing a gun at the two of us.

"Dimitri, what the hell are you doing here?" Leo growled, pointing his gun at the man. "What do you want?"

"Oh, don't act so innocent Leonardo. If you're worried about little Aria finding out, don't worry. All sins will be out in the open by the end of the night," Dimitri grinned maliciously.

"What are you talking about?" Leo hissed. I could tell that he was genuinely confused about whatever Dimitri was talking about.

"Dimitri, let them go they're just kids," Steven came up with his gun pointed at Dimitri.

"And I was just a kid when my father was taken by one of you, but that didn't matter when you did it huh?" Dimitri shouted.

"You don't know the pain of having someone you love stolen from you. My father was all I had, and you killed him!" Dimitri was crying at this point. I felt bad for him but I knew that neither Leo or Steven did this to him. "I tried killing your son in Italy so you would see how it felt, but he wouldn't die. I even hired someone to kill the girl, but that imbecile was useless." Dimitri turned to look at Leo and I, "Maybe I'll kill your father in front of you so you know how it felt."

"No!" Leo screamed.

"Dimitri it wasn't us. Your father had enemies, but we didn't do it. Your father was an ally," Steven tried reasoning.

"You were allies. Not anymore," he turned around, shooting Steven in the chest. I screamed shielding my eyes from the scene.

"Dad!" Leo cried out, watching as Steven's body fell to the floor.

"You son of a bi*ch," Leo screamed, jumping on Dimitri knocking his gun out of his hands. They began fighting, but I carefully made my way over to Steven who was a sickly pale color. I fell down to my knees, putting pressure on the wound.

"Come on Steven, don't give up on me. You can't die. Please, Mr. Moretti, don't die on me," my hands were shaking and sobs were wracking through my body.

"Take care of my son, Aria. Tell him and my wife that I love them," he whispered.

"No Steven, you're going to tell them yourself. You can't leave them. Please, you have to stay strong. Hold on please," I was begging him. I didn't know what to do. "Don't close your eyes, Steven. Please keep them open."

I noticed his eyes move towards the gun that was a couple of feet away, "Save L-Leo, Aria." He managed to get out.

I hesitantly picked up the gun, my shaking hands covered in blood. I didn't even know how to shoot a gun.

"Mr. Moretti, you will live through this. You will be with Sofia, you will not leave any of us. I will be right back, keep your eyes opened," I begged him, getting off the ground walking towards where the two men were fighting. I pointed the gun towards them.

Dimitri was on top of Leo, gun pointed right at Leo's head. Leo turned towards me, his lips turning up ever so slightly. His face was bruised and bloody. His lips mouthed the words, "I love you."

Time seemed to stop. Silence filled the air.

Bang.

THE END

CPSIA information can be obtained
at www.ICGtesting.com
Printed in the USA
LVHW040516140123
737131LV00011B/657

9 781837 618194